MYTH LAB

Theories of Plastic Love

Jack Skelley

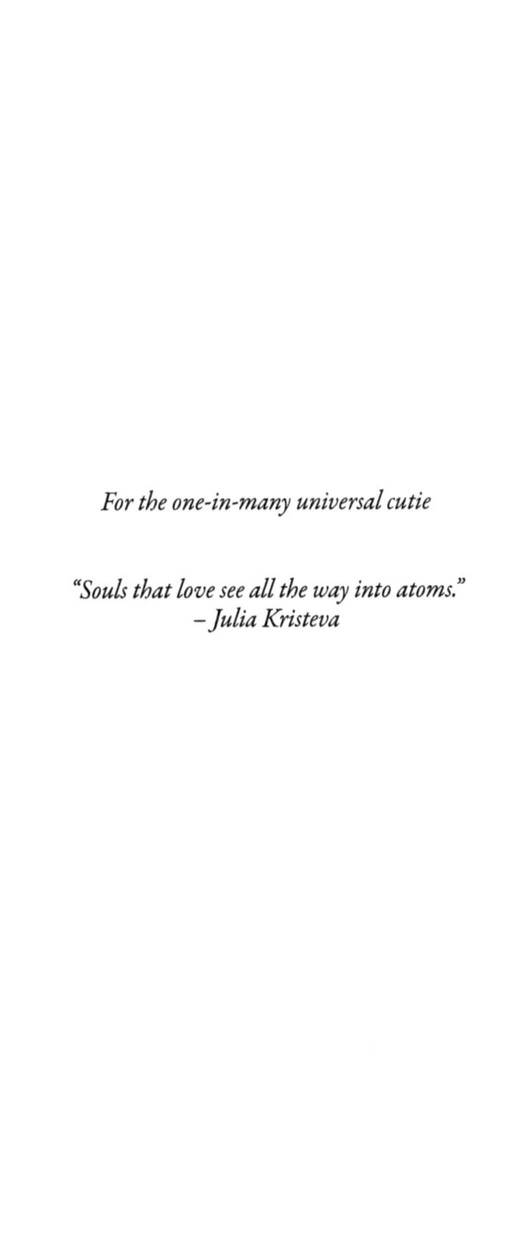

For the one-in-many universal cutie

"Souls that love see all the way into atoms."
– Julia Kristeva

In *Myth Lab*, Jack Skelley adroitly molds an "Einsteinian elasticity between objects and ether" to the "clitoverse." If this formulation seems too vast, just think about a) the last time you felt good about power and b) all the ways to say yes to pleasure as a source of liberation. In conducting "cosmologic psychoanalysis," Myth Lab thrillingly hot wires our neurons to an endless mirror stage reflective of our own instinctual nature.
- Kim Rosenfield, author of *Phantom Captain*

An explosion of clit-cock-and-pop-culture worship. Skelley's eroto-celestial universe fights back not only against the denial of desire – "also known as fuckheadocracy and market forces" – but against death itself.
- Francesca Lia Block, author of *Weetzie Bat*

A hallucinatory book that straddles gender studies, science-fiction, and cultural criticism (to name but three of many genres). Ever eager to use a newfound Skelley-ism, I urge everyone to read *Myth Lab* and be "Kardashian'd" with love (i.e buy it now, it's great).
- Susan Finlay, author of *The Jacques Lacan Foundation*

Contents

Cuties of the Universe

A Species Intervention

How many roads must a man walk down before – face-to-face with his eromantic compulsions, but also infused & enthused with *ecriture feminine* – he manifests an assumption (an elevation of soul & body) into WHIRLING GIRL WORLD? Not until the wormhole ripped the curtain wall of the Vagina Dream Cave Thru Time & Space did I see in Sublime-o-Scope this majorly slurpy suck into the "fuckable crevices of the CUTIEVERSE." Now, here, lofted, I peer into a woman-cult CUNTinent (and then entire Planet) that capsized man-splaining & manspreading of Religion-cum-Rationalism bent on colonizing and commodifying indigenous minds. Instead, this ancient vagilization scientifically empathied a baddass, carnal-powered, and star-faring femme-techtopia. Long before we were Leonardo da Vinci'd, 'twas twats who conquered world-then-space travel. And they infinitely Madonna'd me and Beyonce'd me. They Kardashian'd me and they car-crashed me into sapphire satellites of pure love.

A personal Renaissance appropriating every body, expropriating every border, obliterating every century.

These posts are predictions from that She-ciety, by a lady edge-lord wielding supernatural yet body-based clout.

These are Rebel transports shuttling Lucasian pharmacology to a spectral/spacecraft booty body: Ladies and gentlemen we are floating in space.

Where art classes from a sexy Twilight Zone post a succubus syllabus.

Where before I coveted, cried and yearned, now I learn to teach in these girl galaxies whirled within reach.

Where space bends inward and time drops to its knees.

Where, thru thrashing and blackouts, I grappled with the Otherness of totally wacked-out Girlfriends such as Gidget.

Where same Girlfriend hoaxed me and haunted me.

But now she weaves a garment of stars, a little blackhole dress, spike heels of wholeness, and undies of nothingness.

Where souls that love see all the way into atoms.

You see, before these Amazing Grace incidents, everything was emotional entanglement. As my freak analyst Dr. Tarasoff wrote...

> "He was trying to locate 'real' intimacy in poetry's twin forces: sex and gravitas. Stories of his own and those of friends superclustered writerly complexes, forming, that is, formulating boundaries between vast voids in logic, or memory, the mind traversing its starless expanses as if enterprising to find, and

still doubting, answers to life's big questions, like: where am I? Did that really happen?

"Countless hours were spent calling into the caverns of the night-mind, searching for proof of self in **The Cutieverse**. The laws of physics, like disbelief, are suspended. Candy-coated kisses missed drift in the emptiness of the mind, expanding in the imagination to explode, if only to have someone to call out to, in the darkened starless night, when tormented by the infinite temptation to big bang all the 'cuties of the universe.' "

That is, <u>until</u>... the **Whole Holy Black Hole Love Ho** flowed me. A woman wombed me into the artifice of eternity. She flew me to this: a personal apprehension of Alternate History!

This ultra-She showed me how inner-and-outer space remixed the Hellenic, Mayan, Fertile Crescent Summarian, Byzantine and Indusian caliphates into Dionysus purifiers of femme-formed Platonic/ Gnostic/Kaballic futures. Plus a theological pharmacotherapy of post-pagan mystics:
- Black Madonna,
- Late-century Madonna,
- Like-a-Prayer Madonna, her multi-culti secrecies emblazoned on magnificent boobs, and the letter M tattoos centuries of sky: All AI'd beyond Beyonce in reggaeton or apocalypso menus of every Kardashian implant as realized by some kind of Khalo-Kandinsky.

All these and more – I have learned – edged climaxes of intellect, launching a millennia of Melanias beyond Western societies stuck in death cults of testosterego and denial of women's desire. (Also known as fascism oligarchy plutocracy theocracy fuckheadocracy, market forces and TikTok.)

In, like, a parallel reality, women's soulbodies conquered space and spun our species to the stars. It's a blow-up mystery, so they kinda come off like future-nauts revising all history into one cosmic pun.

These ancient and ageless Cuties of mind, body, spirit: Inclusively, they translated open-source Uranus gods to ventilate earthly and heavenly caves. Both the emotional and scientific conquest of body, now and always, poured language into vessels: not with the mental entrapment of concepts, but thru purity of pictures.

Body of Evidence

Their she-leader launched the bimbo-intelligence-industrial-complex thru post-binary coding of alchemical perfection. Its spells and gospels manifest in digital see-scrolls, newly decrypted to me:

"Europe was in gestation. Our Eastern Queen dethroned political control. Or rather, rethrowned it: An Empress Zenobia, peopling her court with hawt philosophers of cuntology, and multiple brain partners.

"She avatar'd into a 2000 BCE Minoan Crete goddess. Riane Eisler details this in her text, The Chalice and the Blade. *Her bare-breasted style of dress, and for males, the skimpy clothing emphasizing genitals, glorified gender differences plus the kinks they made possible. This created*

a 'pleasure bond' among the sexes, mirroring communal pasts and futures.

"The transcendent rites plus non-rational technology that warrior kings purged and submerged into the ovular oracles of Eleusus survived another 4,000 years secreted on the island of Crete. Its coastal capital of Heraklion was protected by uterus-shaped fornication-fortifications, and on the vaginal walls of the Palace of Knossos were fresco'd rockets penetrating rotational space stations, and divinely detailed maps to the stars.

*"Totally **vagenius**, she twirled and swirled a trans-global amalgam: A Greco-future—that, centuries later, appeared to your Millennials under the influence of dreams, Tarot travel, micro-dosed avocado toast, haunted memes, molly-powered UFOs, and holominds of their own devising.*

"She perceived in a plastic infinity. She conceived the redeeming of creation through desire. A civilization reboot from 'the past,' her femme sexpertise swamped mere male tools through the skin, until – lost to time and hijacked by fate – to the normie world her power seems like phantom, forgotten dreams, an island lost in the eons, or sometimes appearing as ancient astro-shamans... or ET.

"All this really happened. But it happens inside, not on CNN."

Dr Femme X: Endocrinologist as Lascivious Alchemist

And just who was this technocrat queen? This brainy

Titania bish? In "our" space/time continuum she went as **Kate Bush Zambreno** or **Vaginal 'Crème' Davis**. Through the warped prism of network TeeVee she is Star Trek's cybernetically enhanced **Seven of Nine.** (Her full Borg designation is **Seven of Nine, Tertiary Adjunct of Unimatrix Zero One.**) But in the 6th Century CE of this reverse-engineered saga, she is **Empress Theodora**, sailing from Byzantium to alchemize hormonal doorways to desire. Future theorists crown her **Dr Femme X.** This witchy doctor – she called herself **Madame Ovary** – potioned Oxytocin into the cerebral+spinal fluid, freeing erections and sub-clitoral gush. From her Body of Evidence (also a crummy Hollywood thriller starring **Madonna** and **Willem Dafoe**) flourished a vast science of fetishes. A "love hormone" turning receptivity into creativity and transmitting hot-off-the-oral-tradition body memories into torturously sexy yearning.

Majestifed with libidinal energy, she and her proto-e-girl power-minions proved an Einsteinian elasticity between objects and ether. A physics in which matter doesn't matter and **Time** can never catch **Light.** Gravity dissolved into luminiferous space flight, also achieved in lucid dreaming, and pink pocket rockets thrust through dimension portals.

These kinematic Astrogliders tanked up on estrogen. And yet, they could totally bro-out with the dudes. As the **Cynthia Plaster Caster Madonna**-Shaman of the Submerged Cutieverse History, fabricating civilizations with oxytocin and dopamine, Dr Femme X forever showers with gifts the reward center of CEO brain.

There she spins, floats: Augmented in body, mentality

and emotion, exponentialing the species with implants, receptors and empathies of suppleness, this highest of hos holograms signs that peepshow thru the lagging, cock-blocked & gate-keeped war-world of power and brutality that stuns us and guns us.

See? Dr. Femme X swirls before me, iridescing a rose-purple holo-gown of static, resplendent in glitch. She twirls in gifs and glyphs, euphoric phosphenes and a hypnogogic rush in which The Word, as image, is Logos. (Here she predicts <u>our</u> world's media medium Marshall McLuhan's prophecy that thought evolves towards images, leapfrogging language thru "word of eye"). Oxytocin (not its doppelgänger OxyContin!) reigns among her remedies: The "cuddle drug" that makes partners snuggle. A living, breathing octopus-speech pictures sexy elixirs: From climax to aftercare, Oxytocin repositions males, females, remales and all hydra-carnal creatures into this sexy-ass Atlantis. (See: **Kurt Vonnegut's** planet of **Tralfamadore**, home to beings who exist in all times simultaneously; or "Beulah" in **William Blake** who communes there with our **Entrancing Physician Queen**.)

Here she purrs in her long-suppressed telepathic Ted Talk, *Corpus Delicti Delicious*:

"Paracelsus lubricates, potion-lotions and mirrors the chemistry of orgasm, which I, a mercury metal, pour into my container to take shape and make mind. When opposites conjoin, they Burger Queen and Taco Belle a combo-meal menu of each: A hermaphrodite soul union with Luna, where the banished opposite jiu-jitsu'ed back into power and reframed focus. I, as Cynthia Plaster Caster, resurrect Jimi Hendrix in the 27th level of Paradiso, to cast his sweat and jism into molds of metallurgy served on a silver planet that effigies quickcrystal.

"Here: Accept my container of light. It will neoprene you in liquid chromium mental-reflector globules."

And she extends a space-sex suit, comfortably rubbered, made of a here-to-fore unimagined color. And her raiment takes fashion cues from forgotten futures.

"Each bead of goddess jism microcosms you then flows into the whole," she blabs. "Like a daughter of pearl projecting the contents of my mind on my body, I synthesized warm, fuzzy feelings and pro-social behaviors: blind trust, uber-empathy, gazing, happy place memories, bonding cues, and body telekinesis. (You know, like love?)"

For it seems I have learned the S-shaped permeability between lovers in post-coital spooning is the river Liffey winding between waking and sleeping. It is where we spurt & squirt recaptured & half-asleep memories. Where we incant them back to my/our id in a science-dream diary housed on the clouds of moons.

"It was in just such boundary dissolve that engorged clitoral bulbs stardusted the Big Squirt," she postulated via eye-candy pink sigils. These, in turn, spell out the names of lady seraphs and cherubs who patrol the demilitarized zone between time and culture. All this she formulated in her magnum opus, *Language and Its Kink Prosthetics*:

"Sex sounds are gendered. And yet I laughed

uncontrollable rolling orgasms – literal waves of weird words where my magic muff whitecapped again and again, puddling the palace floor with girl-spooge, reflecting the heavens, as when Elf Queen Galadriel (played by cooze queen Cate Blanchett) peers thru her misty moisty mirror into multitemporal star clusters. Their reverse inverse takes shape. That's the **Goddess Cutieverse !!**"

Takeaways: A Cult of Clit Supremacy

The Old World's tired Sartreian myths existentialize us as blank brains cast into matter without purpose; they say we make our own meaning. Sure, that made sense at the time. But now I see that this neglects the egg-like Monad latent inside all creativity, all procreation.

It is said (by Noam Chomsky) that infants are innately tooled to learn every language, until schooled to just the tongue taught at home. Well, from all possible linguals to talking to the tip of her clit, mind and world mingle like mercury and totally based metals. And with our other pharmacological enhancements – smoke, spirits, estro-hallucinogens, pinot grigio, Cialis, Adderall, lotions – I find entire new libraries that undermine Cartesian doubles.

She licks her. she spits his elixir. Rivers of spunk. Cosms of wad and gush. A wide load and a fountainhead.

In sacraments enacted on beds and couches she alchemized a body of restraint, and then scripted that to grunts. The mattress field pulls up roots in deep-throat glossolalia and guttural baby talk. The

Renaissance-to-Baroque presence of the desiring body unbound & rebirthed me, until clit-cults of highly augmented Counter Reformationette sluts shaped a daze of future past and rode to rescue us with boundless blossoms of Rococo bosoms for every body.

In a transitive, contagious rush, we crash the gates of desire to get on the guest list of that part of the soul where the sensible merges hawt e-bitch spirit into supernatural selfies. These skins are crucibles. They are permeable, interior castles. Semi-erect insurgents stiffening into oxymoronic and oxytocic mania to thrust empires of the *cogito ergo cum* within the *corpus mysticum erotocentria* of Julia Kristeva and St Theresa of Avila.

So, now, again, I recall my Mary immersed and Mary emerging. My Marni, Marcie, Marsha & most of all Megan – the most beautiful girl in the world, and I must be the luckiest guy (... sigh...). A borderless woman-made-word unravels her DNA/T'n'A self inside, inundates into places reverbed and digitally relayed beyond matter.

Also now, I think, maybe, I sense even precious-but-tough **CUTIE YOU** revolve and evolve, from hysterical-spectrum elated-in-depression word made flesh, to travels outside of herself, flowing moon tides of images without words into tumults of florescence, a thousand flaming tongues flickering the sad-girl/sade-girl novel of the discorporated e-girl who becomes a golden glowing soul lantern face – like Dante's Beatrice – enlightened from the inside, altering time on the altar of the 1590 Great Bed of Ware. Her larynx throat-singing, gargling, garbling of vocal chords in a tender hate-fuck, are the Logos exploding beyond matter, past the gape matrix, precision-throttling a mental painal stepdaughter channel.

Hers in him, hers in her, hers in thems in hymns of sensation without passive perception, but actively mighty microscoped and magnified into transverberation and inundation.

Fetish Footnote: The Lab Records of Dr. Femme-X

Dear Professor Whorebag—
In response to your visionary research – particularly its evidence that yesterday's **endocrinological crimes** are tomorrow's **brain & body superpowers** – I list a taxonomy of Future Femme Forms. My modified chat doll, muse and eros emanation agencies herself with bolt-ons – far beyond high-profile chatter-bait implants and horizontal junky-trunk booty – to exhibit plump, cock- or labia-pad lips for mouthing and pouting her yummy semaphore. These shoot more synthy pleasure-prosthesis evolvers, including **hormone dosing on a fast-track**. [As noted above – or below, or somewhere between the lines of this document, **Myth Lab: Theories of Plastic Love** – all science, all technology, all culture are prosthetics of language, itself a prosthetic of Imagination.]

This is to overpower then supercharge arousal. A "homely" or "mature" Femme-X variation may mutilate her "liabilities" into gorgeous **dick engorgers, clit swellers** or **cookie-honeymakers**. All true artists understand that ugly is the purest beauty. The butterface being a sainted echelon of angelic skankhood, it milk-shakes and girl-boys itself into body toy: sculpted, bulged, gouged, lasered, tinted, painted. The tension between geometroid and cuboid tits and butts (and other parts) fastened to the chassis – skinny or curvy – achieves her alchemy. And pumped with what? With those solutions of love: **Oxytocin and Dopamine**. The inverse of conforming, this profane **Cutieverse** triumphs over both society and nature. It may replace youth. It may deface and reface itself to please her partner or herself. And in the process, it polymers plastics and emotion elastics into its own reality.

Oh, my daughtered lyrical lovers, pleasuring ladylads, and slenderly elliptical lily liquors, my hot & haughty mamas inflated with dick-and-clit-stiffening orbs of eyes and butts and boobs, inscribe in me, slutastically, your bodily wisdom.

Julia Kristeva's *Teresa My Love: An Imagined Life of the Saint of Avila*, Lotte Latham, Little Soleil, Riane Eisler's *The Chalice & the Blade*, Christine de Pizan, Marshall McLuhan, Sabrina Tarasoff, Afterword to *The Complete Fear of Kathy Acker*, Kurt Vonnegut Jr. Noam Chomsky, *Star Trek Voyager*.

The Clown Dimensions of Uncanny Valley

Carnival Cruises

Ololon* is my emanation. A Sweet River of Milk &
Midnight Whispering. She is a shape-changer from a
river delta, a village by the river, a magnetic resonance
scanned from neurons into speech.

Cloudlike, Ololon whooshes a moonscape. And as
she pours her blessing in floaty drone maneuvers, she
hovers a hand above this carnival, casino, Commedia
dell 'Arte, puppet show or whatever the hell I'm
suddenly looking at, and I wonder: How does a
chemical river, mirroring brain terrain, summon such
entities?

For – Holy Bozo, Batman! – her fine-grained
tinkering opens up to **"Clown Dimensions!"**

When she raises her curtain of eyelids, the below
jesters make their showy entrance:

Parades of clockwork fairies.
Pinhead Pierros and proto Zippies.
Imitation anime ghoul toons sired on the Saturn
of another system.
Wind-up Munchkins on unapproved Adderall
with exoskeletons sequined in zirconium.
Pre-teen splattercore bozoettes.
Fractal-faced tricksters and tykes on bikes who
juggle and jiggle and giggle.
Tons of Teletubby Suns within a raincloud

Titania plopping from a crack in the sky.

I even thought they taught me a snappy Vaudeville ditty titled, "Are You Lucky Tonight?" Until I realized **I was the one free-styling lyrics!**... through Ololon's canyon of liquid song, where rivers and meadows wend and wiggle way down inside.

The Hoax of Doctor Stillborn

In an interpretive stab at **The Clown Dimensions**, Dr Stillborn presents his paper. Among its defective hypotheses is this beaut: *"We humans translate mere electrical pulses into phantasms because we possess innate evolutionary wetware that forces our senses to seize upon any piece of anthropomorphic data that pops from otherwise randomly uniform input."*

Oh, the bogosity!

For starters, this conclusion rests on a binary bias straight outta the exurbs of Normal, Illinois, whereas **my undulating Spirit module** peers into arche-transmissions from Planet XXX. Okay?

Across landscapes of impossibility, they come bouncing. They swoop in front of you, grin, and vibrate. It's all in fast-mo glitch mode: I mean like uncountable frames per second, but each image a pictograph, or graffito, tagged bubble-style on your cranial walls. A worldwide whirlwind of Dewey-decimal catalog cards – each one stamped with a never-before-seen David Bowie persona – flying from the endless drawers of the haunted Central Library, as in some Spielbergian Poltergeist 999... but way better. And other such impossibilities.

My merry machine creatures, bounding down court like self-dribbling Faberge eggs on the rebound, stopped, spoke and joked. From oracles of pouty potty mouths they tried to teach me the reverb of pure verse.

Phhft! Fat chance of that! As all this happened, I barely managed to assure myself that I was even a thing.

"It's okay. Syd Barrett's gnome wasn't built in a day, you know," quoth a man-sized, hydra-headed lawn sprinkler whose 5 nozzles each bore the face of a barfing gargoyle.

Again they come – part goofy mime/part visual words.

> Baggy pants gangbangers named Monkey and Smoky with harlequin hobbit hoodies.
> Pretty boy and girl and in-between goblins in skimpy lingerie.
> The tree-top monkey ancestors of my lower-limbs ape ancestors.
> Slim stick figures but with butt-bumpers, plus swollen protrusions.
> Unhoused and hungry ghosts with no mouths, the shadow people of the underpass.
> White spiders on gummies, smirking as they wack webs of words around us.
> Topless Judy Jetson with 3 perfect orbs, each moon boob bearing triple nipples, doinking heavenward. [DOINK! DOINK! DOINK!]
> Beings made of pure light, and broke-ass shady shamans on molly I wouldn't trust if I were you.

Remember, though: Analogies to Munchkins, Jetsons, Bowie, etc., really don't cut it, because these teeming and fluid entities seem not to settle on any anthropological or even terrestrial signpost. They are Off-World one-offs. Ultra indie movies, not even the 5,000th Marvel franchise. They're mom & pop, not Burger King.

So the question: How may a zazillion entities/ artifacts – rendered in styles not conceivable – possibly register to human eyes while emitted from a non-human source? These are parts of an invisible whole that avoids detection.

Put another way: How in the hell did I see things from an alien dimension where there are literally no such things as "eyes?" Wittgenstein's sphere of the knowable is a tiny bubble these jokers pop from the outside.

The confusion – and this accounts for Dr Stillborn's fucked-up explications – lies in the itchy schism between an object's degree of resemblance to being human and one's emotional response to the object. The more closely yet imperfectly it varies from the known and (previously) seen, the more freaked-out you get.

Therefore, Unlock the Uncanny Valley.

Robotics professor Masahiro Mori ID'd this concept in 1970 in his book, *Bukimi No Tani.*

The beyond-freakish alien escapes our seeing. It straddles the Uncanny Valley between image and meaning. As a product evolved from an unknowable environment it literally is undetectable to human senses. So, as I find myself an audience to these – let's call them visions – that is, to this circus of non-Pantone colors and scrambled grimaces I strain to classify as "clowns," just what am I witnessing? And how?

And still the River Ololon ribbons the Valley in songs.

Think of it this way: Have you ever found yourself spontaneously, almost unconsciously, mimicking another person's phrase or gesture? You may adopt their habit of excitedly replying "Yeah, Yeah!" to a question. Or running your fingers through your hair as they just did. This is a **"Mirror Neuron."** The neuron fires while mimicking the behavior of the other, as though the observer were themselves acting.

It is a mimed joke from **Clown Dimensions.**
We laughed when we viewed it.
We thought we déjà vu'd it.

Lectures at the Linguaversity

And, as the Clouds of Ololon route through this moony world, the river of sexual union dissolves into wet pre-teen dreams.

She sings:

> *I feel his presence flow and mingle through my blood*
> *till it becomes his life and his grows into mine.*
> *In this hydrogen cycle I absorbed vapors when the*
> *sun sinks*
> *gathering the drops my body condensed.*

Turns out its Communions finally liberate the realm

of mature sexual love. Things heard become things seen become inner-felt blurts and blubbers beamed from a geometric-tactile dimension nobody knew about.

This is the "translinguistic glossolalia." (See "Seeing in Tongues" below.)

There is no way in the world the consensus reality of bullet-headed epistemologists can refute these luminous cuneiforms warped in Miles of muted electric horn. An imaginary mathematics that won't figure except for kids & magicians. A couple of universes sitting around talking over genomes.

Visuals are speed-speaking viruses concocted and let loose from some unregulated **Myth Lab**.

Watch/hear fugue lines twist and boogie in my emanation's dimension-adjacent coalition force. She deciphers Sanskrit script rendered in silly string. Worms wiggling with biosemiotics become another pre-verbal surprise.

Then, just when I thought we were getting our groove on, I neglected to prepare a question for my elves. One became hostile and forced me to watch for an opening of Line 23 at the DMV. And I missed my chance to ask the DMT oracle dorks how to translate this here story-thing – **the very text you're reading right now** – into a **Book of Theory**.

But another elf saw me befuddled. Like Clarence in *It's a Wonderful Life*, she took pity on me. She's like a rainbow. She cums in colors everywhere. There she stands, twirly warm in wisdom. A super glitter queen, too. And that medium of flashy deception was her message. Welcoming and whispering arousal bubbles into my ear.

Before you can say succubus, shapely geometrid sisters join her and swarm me too, offering boobs and mouths: "I'm so happy to see you here. Are you performing tonight? Oh, you are? Didn't you fuck Kathy Acker? I'm so excited to hear you read. Come, enter our bimbo boy bubble."

Seeing in Tongues

Soon we – my emanation Ololon and me – learn that the characters of the homunculus clown alphabet are a vaginal form of cuneiform. This explains why the sound-showers of wedge-shaped fractals crack me up.

It suggests that James Joyce's mistress ululates her uvula. It flutters with ovulations in the **"Linguaverse,"** as you might call it. **The ultimate sex worker**, this super uterus is formed by subtracting her slave names from her pet names, and hiero-symbols in double-wide quasar waterways.

Where voice and vagina conflate, you'll find kisses promise more illicit pleasures. The Other's voice cajoles, seduces, instructs, creating the one-hundred-letter word for thunder in *Finnegan's Wake*: (**hunaradidillifaititillibumullunukkunun!**)   And they all drank free at the sky-high open bar. Not in lamentation, but in fuck-yeah jubilance.

And in this Elfin naughty talk, Anna Livia Plurabelle abracadabras a **delta**-shaped, cunny-form triangle, topped at the tip of the tongue by an opening brought to you by the letter "O."

"An ecology of souls dwelling in my back pages became a safe space for your lucid song-dream, the place the music played to me," she tranced.

Or to use engineering terms, we will one day (perhaps today!) display an exteriorizing of the spirit and interiorizing the body. So that the soul shell sheens and swallows as a superconducting lens of translinguistic matter spiraling from the foreheads of each of us.

And, thus transformed, your body image gently subsumes then balloons into a holographic wave, allowing us to float, with Ololon, my emanation, across darkest unobservables and unknowables.

-----

*For Ololon, see: Blake, Milton and Lacan in "The darkness of the nightclub was an airborne aphrodisiac," from *Myth Lab*.

Percy Shelley, William Blake, Terence McKenna, Siena Foster-Soltis, Rolling Stones, James Joyce, Ludwig Wittgenstein, Sabrina Tarasoff.

TikTok Alarm Clock

6

there is no time to tell you everything because they know you are listening but remember trust the man in the red coat standing outside your window he warns you to unlock new possibilities and see new abilities

7

the man in the red coat standing outside your window on August 27 talks truth you can trust however dark binary entities are watching our data so remember the code 0010110 and do not fall victim to great deception when the man in the red coat reveals the truth everything is in place for the last morning be ready and go without fear

13

lizard voices repeat the Second Law of Thermodynamics stating that entropy in the entire universe ever increases over time however you reverse those voices as the universe prefers higher orders of development directing complexity toward our endpoint conceived only in consciousness

22

the time is now my split level ape angel friend for awakening all planes your sacral chakra evolves a universe of intimacy a perfect poem an opera in Arthur Schopenhauer's sense of *gesamtkunstwerk* the structure of creation synchronized in time and *synchpathized* in emotions and *synchpoesied* in that moment of expansion you program the sung and spoken limitless logos and it begins with you my friend

11

between infancy and maturity you pass through prolonged adolescence as language innately folds in gray matter every sexual fantasy fetish and desire to manifest your cravings and obsessions

19

Light Guru scrambles the binary imprisoned Holocaust denier climate denier election denier science denier sexual orientation denier stimulating them to interact with the code 0010110

27

beware the five-year long reptilian shit post will precede a Bot Beast holed up in Macedonian discord boiler rooms serving Dark Mirror reruns to larp scam ram masses duped into doing their quote unquote own research white boomers succumbing to self-flattery claim to be pilled to the 5th dimension but in reality are drunk on normative Brexit and vax memes while zoomers vibe and vape inverting materialism where god particles hear your cries and know your heartache and monitor their human selves in ecosystems ripe for augmenting for the body of humanity receives metaphysical BBLs from digital eugenicists

10

are you in your dream alone or in each other's dreams as content creators swarm to critical mass of data

9

a zoomer with yin/yang face tattoo is your prophet a Post Malone vocalizing mysteries through a harmonizer or a hot girlfriend replika chatbot sending you pussy pics your AR dreamboy holds hands and

coaxes you to pools of pleasure he gets you off the
most flawless actor is sim software for personalized
porn shoots

20

are you ready to meditate 3-19 times a day and
manifest the merge of ultimacy if you remain
imprisoned in hate fear or inhibitions they track you
to fuck you my friend

8

in Hindu heavens 5D resolution replika girlfriends
at 5x speed press lips in pricy intercourse where
influencers eat your feed an AI voice elevates the
comment section to whisper headphone quality
milking and cooing

23

be ready for a Neuralink implant taps pleasure center
responses a recorded chip rewires your partner
and now you feel their genital pleasure throbbing
menus of risk cloak warmth as cortex data meld your
epidermis modified then commodified

16

there is no evolutionary theory my friend without
purpose without teleology without auto particle
theory reverse engineered and future escorted
through intertextual phenomena defined by purposes
not causes thus the contours of evolution approach
the alarm clock at the end of time

3

micro dosed and configured in neural media code
0010110 slipped into a post cubistic now of dreams
& telepathed memetics with 5G Kardashian sexy
baby voice psy-opping in your sleep dropped down

YouTube autoplay rabbit hole in grammatically reversible sentences that make no argument but do scramble synapses

18

gen Z consuming automatically generated content produces false memory and will bring virtual virtues only if you treasure imperfection which is a fictional quote from the electronic baroque as defined by Norman M. Klein

26

time neither ticks nor talks it copulates the most pilled in mimesis of CERN the European Organization for Nuclear Research fucking the largest particle physics glory hole on earth a black hole brains digital bits of compassion into your subconscious feed of adverts during shallow sleep with 24/7 brain brûlée conspiracies and algorhythmically engendered serial mantras of 7 prime numbers chanting

ZERO ZERO ONE ZERO ONE ONE ZERO

5

replaying the Big Bang through Freudian signal anxiety about trauma unlocks love for other people's damage super empaths do this to bloodstream species complexity they speed exponentially as you approach the current moment an asymptotic curve attains a given value a limit called infinity

21

for the cosmos my friend is a curve whose osculating plane at each point coincides with the tangent plane to the surface at that point faster and faster an open-sky akasha epoch will become itself the overwhelming phenomenon that hurries the Mayan calendar countdown

2

remember in 2012 you broke the sound barrier culminating in 100 year moments but you feel the endgame rise inside as a singular moment compresses commotion more vast than eons when nothing happened as the seconds complexify by getting our act together and it invents your present right now my friend

14

forever catastrophe cusping the so called fall of man is the fall into history when consciousness dismembered and disremembered itself as planetary destruction is the plane speeding to the end of the runway it's liftoff do or die if you trapdoor the climate the planet will bounce back but will it rebuild the long road to mind making or will you hurtle off manifold situational cliffs despite semiotic warnings staring you in the face

5

in this prototype dialog AI may suspend climate change by resurrecting community in empathic hunter gatherer narratives for the imagination leading multi and post species conviviality first to understand then modify systems that place our environment at risk my friend

25

you remember your tremendum as your own nothingness in contrast to the terror the near demonic dread absolute unapproachability and monotheist male mass psychosis and hypnosis while your feminizing agent empowers omnipresence through congress with women branded as heretics

4

five times the glaciers ground south from the poles
to smother life and five times retreated so place trust
in you are the prodigal sons and daughters the pride
of a planetary parent because you catalyst coding the
program pressing play on the gambit of hope to clear
noise from communication circuitry

24

the universe coordinates a point of view to become
more self aware of an ever denser shrinking of the
globe and dissolution of political class and gender
boundaries

1

epi-genetic changes are not just biology but
dromology as language and customs accelerate the
mammalian domain to a compassion infused human
machine hybrid every moment essenced by a unique
ideogram or omen token Joni Mitchell's hexagram of
the heavens are I ching hieroglyphs for interplanetary
Amelia Earharts and armchair Magellans exploring
divinatory systems based on 64 subtypes of time and
molecular DNA

12

you have wandered far from your birthright you
have commodified the mystery of being a child if
you don't reverse your virus the cultural momentum
toward lethal conclusion will continue its death
spiral as markets code a finite sequence of rigorous
instructions

15

but angelic direction transmits from carnal realms no
matter what don't forget you are always free always
aloft suffusing both inner and outer space this gets

you off as she inseminates milky ways and cums her
cosmos cream

Q Anon Anonymous, YouTube, Terence McKenna

"The darkness of the nightclub was an airborne aphrodisiac"

This is our perpetual crisis.
The one formed of desire
and its elaborate rationalization, romance.

"The present work is nearer to 'theology' than to scientific or religious history."
– Georges Bataille, *Eroticism*

Arrested for Resisting Arrest

After they'd closed the door and darkened the room, she kneeled, confessed her sins and hinted at the severe penance she deserved. The bad blood between them was a prelude. What had once been a bracing fantasy framed by tactile realities of hair on skin and two bodies sustained by breathing in synch, became one week's petty spats filtered into Saturday night's sex-games.

He found himself letting loose real aggression as he pounded away. And though she had invited this rough treatment, and loved that it made him harder, she still bridled at the good hurt. Pleading for slaps, she'd snarl at the more forceful smacks. This only tightened his grip on her neck, contracting her cunt, massaging his cockhead with internal spasms.

No safe word, but an intuition of when to take a

breather. She'd rise, stomp around like Godzilla in heels, threaten to leave, then relent and resume position: Laid upon the bed-corner altar, her boot-camp-sturdy legs pegged at an acute angle, arms self-pinned. Or, splaying her hair on the pillow, she adorned herself at the headboard, for their bumpiest banging.

Both had wanted more from each other, and now it was all part of a shared state, this anger-love.

She remembers adapting her mother's workout outfit into cosplay: A yuppie cunt snaring the gaze of this pervy art slob. The scooped front and snug straps. The cut-off T that bordered under-boob at the words Venice, California. There she stood, in tight close-up, neon-pink leotard jutting up her puffy wedge. This Pepto-Bismol/Barbie-colored triangle was the apex of leg stems, descending to dipod vinyl cherry-pop heels. The Mission: Keep him mean-hard without him hurting her... too much.

She cooed and rubbed, tugged-up on the elastic. Swung sideways, poked out her butt, pulled up the shirt, pinched her nipples. She pressed her luck, driving him crazy as he lay there, a colossal bone in his fist.

This teasing having reached its limit, it was time to turn the tables. He lept from the mattress and grabbed both elbows, forcibly out-thrusing her torso. Trapped in his grip, she'd squirm and scowl, "Don't touch me there!"

"OK that's it!" She relented only after he flung her back on the bed. Now, triggered into revenge, he took a fistful of hair to leverage her head. To successfully plunger past the pharynx and burrow in the larnynx required him to press his fingers on the base of his cock.

Sir wants tight trachia. That's where Sir is happy. In the the grip of gurgling. Say thank you, Sir.

And again, the greater amounts of pain overwhelmed the game.

Answering Machines

The relationship ended but the story lasted forever.

A fast-paced aggregation of female imagery starts to lose meaning and gender. Essayist and critic Andrea Long Chu defines a female as "any psychic operation in which the self is sacrificed to make room for the desires of another."

The 90s were her glory days. With the skill of a riveter and the intuition of polltaker, she got herself through periods of overlapping girlfriends without a hitch. Coming home with Girlfriend A she'd spy the blinking eye of the answering machine but ignore it until her date hit the bathroom. Once, when she was making out with Girlfriend B on the couch, the phone rang. She knew exactly who it was. Smartly she'd turned down the volume on the machine and it did its job, absorbing in silence the panicked message of Girlfriend A.

I invented her. I wrote her lines. I chose her costumes, her hairstyle, directed her movements—"Oh yes, a nice pout, let your hair fall over your eyes, gaze up at me, now turn around..." Well, she turned around, all right, and fanged the blade toward my chest. She switched scripts to Bride of Fatal Attractionstein. No cartoon now, no compliant lingerie model in my smudged lens. Snow White was Hot Witch, shredding her stuffed animals, and bashing my plaster Madonna on the hardwood floor.

I was so young I could hardly notice myself. I had insights I couldn't remember, and dreams I couldn't explain. Time seemed suspended. The sky was a Cinerama Dome of interlocking bug transistors, vibrating. I saw the Lord from the waist down. Then she appeared, and capitalized on my innocence. Wielding a masculine unity of desires, she knitted a net of fetishes. And whoomp, there I was, swiftly ensnared.

Hear that? He's still there groaning under my bed. From a corner of the room, or medicine cabinet, or one of books he never returned. He's screaming, "You bitch!" But I'm all, "That's right, I'm a bitch and I'm out of here!"

I'm everywhere, I'm everyone. She must murder each of us, one by one. She returns to the scene of a crime that recurs. She sent back my gifts and all photos of me. And yet, somehow, I smile toward her every day.

He will be gone. But.. a corolary voice haunts his house. Not her slathers and moans, but the fuzzy lilt of her tongue in his ear.... Light from the tubes on the ceiling caught the saliva dripping off her tongue.

Down below, too, she was wet. For a price she would obey his instructions, though both agreed there would be no penetration. Knowing just what he wanted, he issued his commands. She was all woman, he complimented, prodding her perfomance. And when his hour was up, she kept it going to get herself off. Afterwards, she considered going out with him.

Mirror Ball

The darkness of the nightclub is an airborne aphrodisiac, a medium fixating through more or less "real" encounters among empaths of mind, emotion and body. At their center is the glitter globe, rotating the room with Saturnian rings. The backlit liquor casements retinge and refract colors room-wide to omni-whirl and infinitize loops of desire. These harmonize into hormonized minds the projections of objects. From personal to interpersonal, in this space the effect is, at heart, not merely encased and enshrined through codes of language, but an "actual" Tantric (skin and breath) experience.

Worming to the bar, I nab a stool next to a figure in mesh top and white gauze sweater. This translucence balances olive green eyes – firm, fixed, peering. These are framed below whisps of doom-blonde bangs: Among the looks of the demimonde, certain styles aspire towards signifiers. Retro-Laura Palmer locks at core may – with the eyes, and clearer than words, say – "I'm free in both brain and body." And as deeper identifications, may declare, "Desires are defined and heightened by the control games, and ritualized force that is the root of human (and only human) eroticism. Succumbing to another's, my will is fulfilled."

She's Helena. She seems to know me. Sure enough, Helena skips all pretense with this ice-breaker: She attends Sex and Love Addicts Anonymous. SLAA. This is not a confession. She's not ashamed. She's based in desire. She goes weekly. She meets guys. Not that she'd ever have trouble getting them. Even now, men hover her hotness. Leaning into me keeps them at bay.

"Some of them are gay," she says. "They want me for friendship. Intense friendship is, for me, very close to the intimacy of sex."

I confess that I too am both of those: A sex and a love addict. Which phantom joy is juicier? This may cause me to "act-out" in hubris, and later cringe-out with insecurities. I can't prevent it. Or I don't want to. Female-embodied opposites somehow elevate into an elastic love, an ineffable core experience that telegraphs as "real."

Reciprocating, I tell Helena I'm a pleasure dom. I lost my partner of five years when Covid hit, and since then I've been searching for a new sub. "I'll be your sub," Helena states. She's on her third Galliano. She presses into me. "Bartender just cut me off." Congratulations! I hand her my Tanqueray and tonic and order another. She asks, "Do you want to put your hand in my pants?"

Because the Mirror Ball is trancing – an encompassing/controlling and crystalline surrounding to a (Ptolemaic) body-universe – it's not until days later I realize that Jacques Lacan has stuff to say about the zone we now orbit. We're totally testing the impossibility of a "real" experience within bounds... both the probing of what we want, and the edgy pleasure of apparitions implied in the seeking itself. *Objet petit FX.*

For some future meeting, we fumble each other's

phones to input our numbers. Her nails are perfect. Thin, pink almond-shaped gels. I fucking love manis. In this case, it's fair to catalog them too as signifiers. A manual alphabet. A body language that self-interprets. Elongated, shaped, buffed, glittered and – outrageously – elaborated with mini 3D dioramas of butterflies, flowers or Sanrio characters, these fingernails say, "I ransom dexterity to the charms of artifice. Watch me press my keypad with the ball of my index finger – the distal phalanx, itself an index of arousals – the length of nails forcing fingers to display themselves, like bare, out-stretched legs. Not that this is an invitation. In fact, it may denote a level of **autoeroticism** more than a need to attract others. But you can't help fantasizing this tactile elegance (formed by the faith of spirit) in the act of touching. Imagine these acrylic tips lightly scratching the veins of your elongated cock, or pinching the swollen hood of your clit, depending...."

I type "Hi Helena." Heart emoji, spark emoji. She replies "I love you and I want you." Since she's offered herself as my sub, I explain how I "kiss" my sub: I molest their mouth, take it. Then and there she yields it. We're deeply tonguing. Or, more accurately, I pry the lips and overtake that hole. Own it. To leverage probing, I cradle the back of her head.

It's dark in here, but I'm sure people see us in action. That's embarrassing, but why? Eff 'em, says the Mirror Ball.

She wants more. Though I'm the one nominally in control, <u>she</u> guides <u>me</u> to the mens room. There's no lock on the door but there's a toilet stall and we lock that. I press her against the wall, but she doesn't need much direction. She complianty lifts her blouse. There are her boobs. Magnificent. She's proud to proffer them. "Push them out. Arch your back, arms behind you." I slap them. I slap her face. Affectionate-firm, with force. Again the mouth molestation. Fingers and thumb gripping neck and chin. She'll give me anything. I slide my hand down her pants, swirl her clit on the way to her cunt. She's moaning. She's wet enough to squirt. I alternate the press, scoop and twirl, tenderly in synch with breath and heartbeat. She's cumming. Now she drops to her knees. She's going to blow me. That's when I stop her. Somehow, despite the liquor and ego intoxication, despite the air of eros we gulp in pants and groans, I default to reason: People know we're in that stall. Even if they're not peering through the crack, they hear our transgressions. I lift her from the floor. I assist in reassembling her white sweater, but it's hopelessly tangled around her arms and shoulders. We return to the bar. Suddenly, amid the crowd, she's gone.

Bataille says, "Once the transgression is permitted, it is often prescribed." And so, because I halted our transgressions, for hours afterwards, Helena's pussy tang annoints my fingers. I won't wash it off. It is a window to larger worlds...

The Mirror Ball revolves. At its chrisanthemum center is the passion of Helena: un-encrypted, unbounded, elevated. Orbiting. A love anima. **Scriptured in gush**. An embodied and femme'd language. Alive to both inner and interpenetrative relations. In what may seem a craving for flings, I sense as **a soul at one with the substance of life**. While her blessings of physicality are the vehicle of her quest, her heart is her attraction. The feelings she returns exteriorize the spirit and interiorize the body. You can see it in her smart and archly ironic smile. In the mix of self-confidence and self-consciousness. And the bangs, the nails, the glassy gloss and gauzy top, (another time we can talk about shoes)... these enhancements are "just" proxies for biology, and yet they unlock into herself – and fleetingly into me – an evolution of being. An individuation.

The fierce desire of this cutie bubbles up from consciousness warped/wrapped in the sacraments of body language. The crystaline spheres of a girliverse reflect in her flesh, by way of compulsions, an oracle, an exaltation... which is a kind of hot divinity-in-humanity that circles into the everything.

A Language of Worms

Then, with each breath, she tasted her bronchioles – the cul-de-sacs of lungs – slurp sweet/tart, Galliano-like love-liqueur into her arteries. Her past, proscribed by catechisms of sardonic, post-second-wave-feminist memes, fluttered away like childhood, while her future flooded with Yosemites of sex/affection addiction.

And, on the third day – the prime number of time's triangulation – I rose again to a verbal world infinitely fertile in suggestions. Every object in this world can pass from a closed, silent existence to an oral state, owned by all who mouth it, morphed by all who use it.

In what wrinkle or bowel of my cavities are the ashes burned millennia past? In what oozy ventricle of the ocean is the jelly of a body drowned in the general flood? In what cave lie the remains of my Neanderthal dad who died – by the evolutionary clock – just yesterday?

But always waiting is what? A worm, a weed, an ant, a spider, a toad and a viper? All circle into meaning, then recede in revolutions of dust. They are bold and everlasting worms, which after skin and contents are destroyed, remain, as the gods remain, gorging on consciousness. They are the "abject horror" that (as Julia Kristeva posited) confronts the materiality of my sexuality.

And George Bataille reminds, "When the bones are bare and white they are not intolerable as the putrefying flesh is, food for worms…. Desire is only aroused as long as its object causes a chasm no less deep than death to yawn within me."

As my body battles age, the worms beg: Feed us the infinite atoms that black corrosives gnaw. The limbs I long to hold. The desire that drives complusive search.

Yearning for a future polysexuality recalled by Aristophanes in Plato's *Symposium*, self-cloning becomes a cellular dream. At least now I can imagine Artificial Life reproducing itself, loving itself.

So I enter the language universe of visual signs. Of the many worms of speech, be they photos, movies, memes, reporting, sports, plays, publicity – all are ordered and destroyed by meaning, crawling through tunnels, thought fending off rot through veins of eroto-philia.

The minor-key chapters: Drowned loved ones and betrayals by lovers. Darkly devastating & emotionally bracing scripture-verse – which plumbs the catastrophes of loss – emits beeps from a lost satellite, rivers of tears and midnight panics, even as I – love junkie – grapple to recapture that first, sweet admixture of love and sex. I still feel it in my teeth and bones.

That mind-body-swirl of boundary-dissolve.

Aftercare

I strain to clearly understand/confront the psychosexual dynamics of my "acting out" by placing them in cosmological terms. The Pussyverse. I swirl-swim there. It is life. The love for women (and men but mostly women and why is that?) swerves from **overwhelmingly emotional empathy** (an addiction) to bodily desire and back again. I listen. I want to know their stories. Their lives. How they hurt. What they want and how that makes them who they are.

But – no surprise – it turns out it's hard to separate this mostly positive ecstasis from the acknowledging/confessing/glorifying of my most fucked-up kinks. How awareness of the kink – e.g. for the "false," materialistic trappings of dress and makeup – becomes a kink in its itself: Commodity fetish as actual fetish. How it makes me hard to hurt a her who wants me to hurt her. How I yearn to hold and heal. How, upon cumming, I laugh uncontrollably. How, later or at any time, I weep at the most maudlin nonsense. A detergent commercial.

And now I think my neediness inspires a new piece called, "Aftercare LOL." And just who is comforted more: me or her? Who needs it more? Are these feelings the rumblings of beautiful cunt-souls?

Your soul. I hear it. It's beautiful.

Acting Out

Before we meet he asks me about limits, but he is being shady about the narrative. He wants me to wear a mask while he videos a family-type threesome. With me as his ex's "money grubbing" daughter. Apparently, I look similar to her? Does he plan to upload the video as some kind of fake revenge porn. Is he trying to set her up?

In deciding whether to take the gig, I get distracted by "research." I give myself two orgasms watching videos with titles such as *"Stepdaughter will do anything for money."*

It's not the DDLG of it that makes me wary. It's his barely concealed tone of aggression describing this young person he wants to smear. I worry about being complicit, but I'm attracted to violence. And... why is that?

The night arrives. At the Biltmore, I speak into the voice recorder: My name is Marni, my safe word is "more," and I consent to being here.

He holds the leash in one hand and his iPhone in the other. I circle the furniture on my hands and knees. His "wife" is waiting. Suddenly, she starts calling the shots. She commands him to sit on the sofa. I face him on my knees.

Call him a dirty, cheating piece of shit, wife says. Did I say you could move? What a good little slave, wife says.

Is this what you want? Wife yells at him. You knew I'd find your dirty texts! I will put a tracer on your phone, piece of shit!

She keeps the pressure on me as well. How much money did you steal from us, Marni? What did you spend it on? Drugs again?

Now it's time for you to take your punishment, Marni: No! Stay on your knees. Put him in your mouth.

He stands and presses his cock into the back of my throat.

You like that?

My throat is trained from experience and enthusiasm: At the proper angle I can fit a full 8 inches. Especially "head over bed." But I won't do that position: Too much saliva running into my eyes.

Are you having fun? she says to me on the side. Okay good, me too. This is so good!

Now, Marni, get the lube.
Get on your back. Now!
It's time to DP.

If I'm in the right mood, I don't even need lube. And whatever pain I feel can be a turn-on. This is one of those times. I could have taken more. But he got too drunk and lost his erection.

Afterwards, in the elevator down to the lobby, I check my email. I have appeared in a casting search for a "runaway daughter."

Craniotomy

Hi!

First off, my apologies for not replying sooner. I read your letter many times, and I felt so much of it, because you are very open in your writings.

I long for more conversations about your life now, my life now, and what the future looks like.

You have meant so much to me, more than you know, more than I understood at the time.

I tried to keep everything professional, but we crossed that line early on. And soon I began thinking about you, and our times together, and looking forward to our next meeting. I felt safe with you. You helped my heart open up. And though we've become separated, you are in a special place in my heart. No one can take that from me.

It felt good to trust someone again, laugh, reveal myself, and each meeting brought me closer to you. But we never shared that most important truth, did we? I understood your situation and would never put you in a position where you felt like you had to "do" something about it. I simply expressed my joy, sharing pieces of my heart.

But you remember that time we stood facing each other. Without saying anything, I gestured what we both felt: I pulled my heart from my chest, cupped it in my palms. I handed it to you. You accepted it.

I can't tell you how many times I longed for those nights. Unfortunately, my health took a bad turn and I have been trying to gain ground again ever since.

The Neurologist got back to me regarding my MRI and Xray...it doesn't look good. There is pressure in the left frontal lobe that is bigger than he would like it to be ....so I have been referred to the Neurosurgeon. It's crazy. This doesn't seem real to me, but it is very real. There are 3 options.

> 1) Keep an eye on it
> 2) Radiation
> 3) Craniotomy... That is, brain surgery. To remove the growth.

Overwhelmed is putting it lightly. I would love to find a way to meet and discuss.

Thankfully, I have the best insurance. I pay zero for all my medical and dental. Plus a great psychotherapist!

Voluptuary

Each meeting is defined by ritual. As I grab the ice and crank the tunes, she extracts items from her "Daddy bag" and lays them on the bed. A selection of outfits. A string of tiny lights which I drape over the bedposts. Candles, a few large ones plus a smattering of votives. The leash. And a choice of 2 collars with studded lettering: "DOLL" (pink) and "SLUT" (black). Black cuffs.

We unfold a protective sheet across the sofa. A stack of towels. Pillows on the floor before the sofa.

Lights dimmed, she begins a series of touch-ups in the full-length. More gloss. Adjustments of her outfit. Posing. Pouting. This gets her off. She loves to make herself as hot as possible. She keeps her heels on because she knows, from the first time I saw her, that I like it. And not "pleasers," aptly named for some but not for me, but rather, my preferred pumps.

And yet, all this is less to please me than herself. This self-adoration. Early in her transitioning to (a bodily version of) female, she explains she best understands herself as an **autoerotic**. She gets off on observing herself observe herself. Not in the sense of internalizing or gauging her attractiveness, the way some women say they are hyper aware of how others see their bodies. Or not just that. For, as she fixes herself in the mirror, it's clear she worships the body she has altered: manufactured for fucking. Less to arouse her partner (male or female) than herself. I stare at her staring in the mirror. She rubs and strokes. Does she peer through "the male gaze?" Is it a female filtered through the male or the male through the female? Or triple layers of the two?

And yet, with her, I could never misgender, or confuse pronouns. She is always "she." Even though she has retained her cock.

Enough of this: I command. She kneels before me.

These are the rites of the un-making of ourselves, the desire in symbiosis obliterating all bounds: from flesh to morality to temporal reality. She inflects her dark brown baby-doll voice, "I want to worship your cock... I want to worship your balls... and I want to worship your ass." A Naughty Emanation: Whoretoy who dons the collar, a girly-girl princess sissy bitch with painted eyes and bleached extensions waits in place to smear her face, crawls, offers her hole. Good girl. Daddy rubs around her entire head and snugs into her face place. "Fuck my whore-hole, Daddy, please."

Get it in there, all the way down … now, eyes on me!! Now cross them. Look up at Daddy and what do you say, slut? Giggle girl will slobber thru her Daddy hole like a drippy cunt. Garble and gurgle yes Daddy again and again till Daddy says to stop.

Each encounter she elevates another notch with atmospheric fetish wear and skimpy, sheer word/images. Meanwhile, she continues her body modifications. Selfishly, I support her extreme variations on "brainy bimbo" prototypes, affirming yet disrupting standards of beauty.

The Ladyboy model is ultra hot in this obliterative way. She's augmented everything but retains the cock, attaining more fake/real contrast – an uncanny valley of the body – and ever-increasing ratios of aperture to protrusion.

And there's a plus in such femmies: An interiorized and radiant sluthood transcends whatever the body's got going. A desire to appease its need to please itself.

"I was born this way," I used to say.

I searched with many partners. All were enlightened souls. True beauties. Saints in ways that men can never be. Just one was able to provide not only what I need but anticipate it. Sacramental. Mind/spirit meld. Time stopped. Every encounter more risky…

She knew me more than I knew me. Terms like role play don't come close to capturing it. Towards the end, we were on the verge of gratifyingly dark anti-gravity. Of suspending then reversing time into a co-hallucinatory, oxytocin-fueled tunnel felt through our pores. Of edging, cumming, edging and cumming again.

And then... I lost her. I had my life. She needed safety and security. Withdrew. Found support. Disappeared. I supported her decision. But these have been painful months, overlapping with the burst of emotion- and memory-driven writing I'm undergoing. Reconnecting with old friends and lovers. Can you explain how that works together? Memories unearthed. Love lost. Intense creativity. There have been recent turns in this story. Half elated, half dreadful. Fateful. She re-emerged last month. But we can't be together. The brain tumor is scheduled for removal.

Factors combined to plunge me into a severe depression – one of the worst of my life. Where you yearn for the annihilation of sleep. You dread the nightmare and the day despair, the moment of waking-up because it's there again, staring you in the face. Compulsive thinking, a scratched and broken record jerking back to the beginning of itself. Or one of those nightmares with false endings. The ones you can't wake up from. Panic.

I questioned my life. My values and behavior. The deep shame. Sleeping & eating were accomplished small bits at a time.

The loss came in layers. I probed it with my therapist, and my new European friend. She is a super empath.

She helped me pull out of it. She gave me a list of books about grief. Books that helped her through similar crises. I read half of them.

In Maurice Blanchot's *Writing of the Disaster*, "Disaster always already happened." The grief, though I try to hide it, is public, part of a network of dream-logic disasters. What most writers ignore in their inward-obsessed memoirs is that loss shatters not only the self, but everything around. And a person then finds themselves wishing for death. The completeness of obliteration.

"To die is to embrace the whole of time and to make of time a whole. It is a temporal ecstasy. One never dies now, one always dies later, in the future—in a future, which is never an actuality, and which cannot come when everything will be over and done."

Extra-Sensory Kinesthesia

1. 15 days to go? Is it Oct 7? Please tell me the exact date. I will pray, manifest, and envision success that day. I will send all the mental support I can "through the ether," as you say. I maintain a positive attitude about the outcome. And I wish the best for you every single day. I know you feel like you have to "wrap up your life." But please keep affirming. And I will too.
2. I understand you're off-the-charts anxious and afraid. And this is affecting your focus. That is to be expected. From what I can tell, you are handling a very alarming situation in the best ways you can. Whatever feelings you have about it are valid.

3. And your positivity is helping – even though you may not feel it. Your inner strength will also help you heal afterwards. I support you. 100 times over.

4. I have one very close friend with whom I discuss your situation. Extremely compassionate, intuitive and sympathetic. A real artist. She understands the history you and I share. (She's going through her own extreme difficulties right now as well... I often send the both of you strong ether vibes on the same days and hours!!) I told her how you are frightened of disfiguration. She thinks this shocks or scares us so deeply because our relationship was founded on a physical bond. She uses the word "proprioception." It is your body's ability to sense movement, action, and location. It's the erotic kinesthesia that we shared. It's how we "knew" or intuited elevating sensual pleasure into mind-melding. Now Eros the god of sexual love turns to Agape's compassion. I mean, I still treasure all our adventures. But, because they transcended our bodies, I feel an almost impossible empathy for you. I sense you in the ether. It's very moving to me.

5. It is Love.

Freeze Mode

During the trauma of rape, they instinctively went into freeze mode. Now they fetishize then neutralize that trauma by reenacting freeze. This involves pain but, paradoxically, it's also comforting.

Their submission to their Pleasure Dom reframes the

pain into safety. It is also exciting. PD understands their need for this inverse giving and receiving pleasure through restraining, controlling, choking, spanking and other "good hurts," which, during coitus tightens her cunt, offering PD even more pleasure.

On the phone, they and PD verbally rehearse their next meeting. To introduce new games, they watch timestop, hypno, stuck or robot porn. They have long chats and aftercare sessions with their PD about direction and boundaries. They crave instruction. Forceful commands. Each command is more difficult, the poses more straining. PD becomes more firm and forceful. But PD does not yell at them.

They are told to strip down to their underwear. They are told what they've done wrong. Their penance involves their arms gathered behind their back, held firm, upright, ass-out, for spanking. Slapping. Probing.

They're wet and getting wetter with each slap. They don't know when the next slap will hit. Or if PD will instead shove a hand into their cunt. Their cunt is the center of attention. The center of all sensation. They're a wet cunt. That's what a good slutty whore is for.

When PD yanks down their panties they are embarrassed. Standing, wrists gripped. Now their entire body is exposed. PD kicks their legs apart to scoop deeper. They cum over and over. They squirt on the floor.

FOOTNOTE:

Blake, Milton and Lacan

The mind rationalizes lust to love. This deception showed William Blake, possessed of deep compassion, how women were treated in this world and the resulting hostility of women toward men; how the feminine principle could cooperate and reclaim its rightful role. Milton's *Paradise Lost* showed that Milton did not acknowledge the equality of women with men. So, in his epic poem *Milton*, Blake had Ololon – his "emanation," an erotic alter-ego and feminine muse – descend in Milton's path to accept her involvement in the estrangement between the divine and the human and try to correct it. The male and female share the redemptive process of integrating the psyche with itself and the sexual universe.

A cosmologic psychoanalysis, this process is a neverending now.

In Jacques Lacan, is "the big Other," which represents otherness itself, the object cause? The internal prime mover? Is this the force that induces desire towards the object? Yearning for the thing, versus the thing itself?

The "other" (*autre*) moves in the same direction as Blake's concept of "emanation," or imaginative self-identity. In Blake's prophecy of *Milton*, the emmantion of Ololon is a river, the commuity that lives by the river, and the linguistic cave from which the river flows: a "sweet River, of milk & liquid pearl," the lifegiving river of Eden — blended genders and undifferentiated sexuality. The milk of women's breasts and the pearly semen of the male.

Kim Rosenfield, William Blake, Lotte Latham, Northrop Frye, Lily Lady, Jean Baudrillard, Kathy Acker, Julia Kristeva, Gabby Sones, Andrea Long Chu, Maurice Blanchot, Sabrina Tarasoff, Madeline Cash, George Bataille.

Rendezvous with God-MILF

The Exposé :   Transvestigation Revelations

Many if not all public figures deceive the genders they were assigned at birth.

This video proves that Michelle Obama is a man who presents as a woman: Hands, shoulders, genitalia, frozen face and "female" hairstyle, carefully structured wardrobe and distorting smile. Just before her death, 81-year-old Joan Rivers announced Barack Obama is gay. For this, Joan Rivers was murdered by the Obamas!

We exhume Cleopatra to suck their ghost penis: Their Adam's apple throat bulge proves to be better hung than me!

But what about celebs already claiming transgender status? They are double Trans! Caitlyn Jenner is a woman as a man as a woman.

Every politician. Every photo portrait stamped with a Getty watermark. Every famous person today and throughout history is EGI: ELITE GENDER INVERT.

Ariana Grande's HRT business was her entry to stardom !

Beyonce has a male digit ratio !

Natalie Portman has straight manly clavicles !

Ronald Reagan has misplaced necrotic nipples !

The Avastars

BUT wait, now, these celebri-mutations guide a great leap. Not by genetic adaptation but by **evolution of the <u>concept</u> of biology** will come (and I'm not shitting here) **the conquest of time and space.** Transplants, cosmetics, and HRT jump-start the acceleration of the race. And gender dysphoria unravels to gender diaspora!

The Digi-Scripture: Apocalypse Mom

I
The Singularity of Infinite Plurals

With the advent of the sky saucer mandala, your personal celeb/trans menage de beaucoup annihilates time through sexstasy!

Blow-up your pronouns, dim earth-normies. Under evolution-omics, euphoria puffs multi-person plurals: Here in the Great Gynopolis, each party's gravity grip and rubbery lips suck the polymorph of **Time**, and glint like string-theory party lights: One life with many peacock eyes popping open the glorious **Overhole**.

Gender particles – like galaxies – resist parsing. Pronominally, "him" or "her" are more Q than A.
- Are you me or am I you?
- Do I suck you or do you pump me?
- Was what's thrust FROM the past actually yanked TOWARD the future?

I can't push it out without pulling it in, they said on the bed, arms pinned overhead. In this reverse engineered Big Bang, species complexification is not shoved from an origin, but towed towards a pre-ordinated future: Not growing outward but gathering inward towards a single completion.

> These antics instant-replay to advance eros itself.
> Hormones are the third person of the Holy Trinity
> And the tenth man in the stands.
> The boulder-busting Easter in her heart darts into big-ass data.

That engorged weapon that pierces the martyr's skin outlines "original sin" on the cave wall – twin shadows where one signifies itself and coincides with the other.

The next sexual position for the body engaged in this three-way is union with the other two. Now, transpose this triad to a higher key: Tranify one augmented male with the parts of all three partners, and peer thru ruby-glitter layers of celestial celebrity.

Mother Beloved appears in sticky stained glass. The chaste bride's moan and harlot's curse is *Prima Materia* – it only matters the first time, when the chaos of everywhere poured into vessels of contradictions and colors. (As described in Jung's *Mysterium Coniunctionis*.)

I press the tremolo bar **bending notes of Time**.

And, ah! My Sister Brother and Space Ghost Host, **epigenetic alteration** is no longer a biologically based but a linguistically based pink triangle mystery upthrust and untucking the high-thread-count sheets of mother-matter, once housekeeper-tight, as yearning casts bodies past adolescence into a meta-human who sucks androgyn quarks, forever unfolding and – oh, ladylad! – beautiful to behold.

II
My Constellation Glamazon

Skimpy yet cloaked, was she radically normative cis-het, or hot trans tail trailing scent? Were her bronzed contours so ALL-CAPS to advertise jism cosms of divadom? Ditto the starry fat black lashes, thunder booty, ruff-tuff creampuff shoulder-to-clavicle ratios, and anti-gravity ultra-high-projectile lunar boobs... these bookending a grande Mariana Trench proportioned to slot phalli or interlocking pairs of nymph nips.

Then there was her dark brown voice: That gravelly laugh came from the brain freeze of chugging beers and huffing galaxy dust. (Chokey weed, for sure, but I never saw her smoke a cigarette.)

Oh, such sweet disorder in the mess.
Were the obvious cosmetic surgeries rip-offs or tip-offs?
Was the bimbo/himbo confusion boyish, girlish or combo-pack?
Was that dummy dolly act for him or herself?
For when Lola croaked her throaty coaxes, my Ray Davies inside just about died.

You see, as technology dissolves barriers between mind and machine, extremities of artifice spiritualize and sexualize matter. A malleable mystic persona doll is peak plastic power.

(As Joris K. Huysman's *Against Nature* creamed to the perfection of fakeness, "He had done with artificial flowers aping the true; he wanted natural flowers imitating the false.")

Try to envision her skin. Two highly attractive blackholes swap spit in a death grip. We don't see them: They go AWOL from our electro-spectrum, with its noted human bias. Now, however, the hands-on analysis of Mary Mammoplaster Caster confirms Einstein's far-fetched concept of "**gravitational ripples**." It's a Cosmetological Cosmology. It works like this: The epidermis stretches over a set of swollen orbs. This creates wrinkles and waves (not particles) which softly klink and krinkle in up-cupped fakey shapes. These perfect fabrications bolster and upholster a stick-figure in the stars. If you connect the skinny dots into a come-hither constellation, the silicone domes orbit whore ports of magnetism.

A ruby fingertip tugs at a pout just out of collagen college. And really, any surgery scars, visible hair-weave, every botch or mutilation – indeed all crow's feet, neck lines, knuckles, stretch marks and poking-out clavicles – canonize her. They are Andromeda's exquisitely rotten fruits, beatified.

Among a bazillion Brazilian butt lifts, only hers are outfitted with nipples, and these spin towards ethers of spheres.

Ah, my supreme drag-décor Queen embeds in glam gloss: Magnify her godhead.

III
A Neurodiverse Universe

Wild animals entering the neighborhood are celebrities. A racoon moonwalked and twerked along my fence. Likewise, aliens are big stars who – once you learn their language – open all their holes to the happy mishaps of your synapse crackle and pop.

Take Saint Dymphna – meta minx and mother nymph. She is the martyred patron of...
- sluts
- sex workers
- runaways
- hyper-emos and super-empaths
- self-hating narcies (inverse narcissists)
- impulse-pervs
- the trauma'd and the triggered
- paranoiacs and pronoiacs (for whom the world conspires to do them good)

Asperger kings and queens are so hawt in bed! Amping their psyches on the whiplash and curlicues of neurodiversity, these **Sur-Spectrum Art and Love Warriors** rise from compassion to tactile telaesthesia: Yes, they feel what they arouse from afar. See them soar through their minds in ADHD Superfocus: Their self-critiquing traumas fog a butterfly effect past boundaries of skin and space.

Next, picture the melding of medications, genes, hormones, and surgical implants (both silicone and silicon), cross-faded not with just booze and pot, but chemical neurotransmitters such as psilocybin. For what is an angel but an ape seriously enhanced?

But what if your quasi-quasar secret-crushes snag the hems of their gowns on the great, circular escalator of being? That is, what if you're stuck in tight nightmare spots of anxiety where you pump and pump and pump the brakes, bones to the floorboard, but the dumb bus won't stop?

Relax, babe: Just shove her in reverse, and invert your sex. Those freakouts are but flimsy Ikea particle board. And today's your lucky eon, when the unmoved Omnimover – the biggest Mom & Pop operation in the universe – downshifts the heaviness of time to mere tense. **Words are a projection of desire and grammar is emotive.**

For when it comes to trauma, the issues are in the tissues. Doctor Porno College recommends crumpling your event horizons into strange bedfellows. A goo-fuse of intersectional secret passages speeds and exceeds the gravity of others, perfecting the desire to explore space – inner to outer, weightless to timeless.

IV
The Kink Kontroversy

If DNA is evolution's hardware, language is its software, and dirty talk does most of the coding.

A demigirl and demiboy fell in love, rose in lust, and double-lutzed their binaries into strawberry Twizzlers before plateauing (creaming and screaming) upon each other like gods of smut.

Our Mary of the Immaculate Conception, The Overhole, pink-collared her subby cosmonautress, roped her like a revolving moon. Buoyed by Queen-of-Heaven cougar coos, this messy miss emerged from 40 minutes of forced Hitachi orgasm to make delicious space moan upon an apex at perpetual midnight.

In just this way you may telescope your libidinal hourglass figures and fondle history's prettiest pop stars who slink in sequins and warble a **Dolby Doppler effect**.

Now go get yourself a nice warm love ghost named Dolly or Lola, one who cozies you in 500 spiral-galaxy arms. One who intuits your kink before you think. One whose celluloid-to-celestial apotheosis squishes sweet juices from your fondest adolescent imprintings.

V

Stupid Cupid & Sexy Psyche

The telepath composes an Ode to Space. This pimps-out her God-MILF in the same Eros LEDs as those adorning the Milky Way bar at the galactic Rainbow on the Strip.

In such a setting, Psyche is so naturally glam that jealous Venus orders son Cupid to make her fall for some bum on the street (yes, even a low hobo like you). But as soon as he catches sight of Psyche, he wants that yum. He drools for cum. And – accidentally on purpose – clumsy Cupido catches his own arrow and falls hopelessly for Psyche.

Zoom cut to room 565. Secreted there, they harmonify their rendezvous to climb inter-bliss moments that burst.

    - He masks his face.
    - This carves pathways of neuro-emotion emissions.
    - They don't dare speak the word "love."
    - He covers her car payments and storage-unit rent.
    - In exchange, she does his chart and gifts him smoky smooth crystals to be placed upon the windowsill when the moon is full. These, too, manifest their desires.

Our **Fuck-Mother-of-All-Holes-Church** houses their unutterable passion between sundown and turn-down service. Her manicure twirls the dumb angel Cupid around shining soul Psyche and they swirl up **heaven's whorearchy**. Psyche achieves ultra-empath mistress guru status. She finally grabs a glimpse of his face. And there throbs his true heart.

They mutually masturbate a Ring Cycle of celestial love, where chromatic waves crest and never resolve – an endless "almost," ever edging on her wet wedge. She Tristans her oracle ovals, docking with his morning rock, stiff yet weightless, as if crafted in titanium sourced from the silver moon that orbits the moon of Titan, (which orbits Saturn, of course).

Ah, seraph of lashes and leashes. Ah, dramas of punishment and reward that are a lesson to us all. Intermingled in light, this feeling couple quivers pearl necklaces of knowing!

VI
Luvpocalypse Now

The mattress is a continent. Desire is self-invention.

Theia was the ancient planet who collided with earth to make **our Mother the Moon**. Today, she throws the book at dualities of a someday soon. Plus, if you act now, totally gynodelic jams re-mix your genitalia. They purr and boom with funhouse fluids.

The past gets lonely. It smothers your momentum. But here, in the instantaneity of sensation, there is no later, dude... just the presents of your presence.

In acts of insurrectionary physics and metaphysics, clandestine appointments ripen into a roleplay so refined it melts their mind. Side by side, They act as wombmates. They yearn and turn, her cock swelling, his dilating heart a gash of gushing girl juice, spent yet bursting, as in the Doctrine of Plenitude traced by Arthur Lovejoy in *The Great Chain of Being*.

And lest this incest-play insufficiently arouse you, her Seven Sisters, the Pleiades, are open to a 10-way.

Alchemical weddings of alien entities with titties chronicle insect gods with replacement parts. This is LUV relations — I am she and you are we and each party grabs each other together.

Till they became what they beheld.

VII
We, Robot

I, **Space Gaia Overmind**, through carnal upgrades, will now take your order: another round of estrogen energy cocktails for everyone!

Have no worries, babe, about the shape of things

to come. Remember, in apostolic eras, We, the first Millennials, eating avocado toast from food carts on the Appian Way, also feared that imminent end times were today (100 CE). Then – out of the blue! – Our gospel scroll gets a publishing date from future publisher-creatures made of data. Like the end of Ray Bradbury's *Fahrenheit 451*, after they burn, we turn into the books we love. And our personal search history becomes epic verse of souls and holes.

Hey, **Animama**, tarted-up on pills and pillow-talk, but bogged down by past trauma, come inside and confide in your **Holemother**.

In a baller **Red Queen** move, let **Our Cougar Princess** re-emerge as a C-3PO monad prototype, buoyant with boobs, dong and **a voice of the velvety Vulva**.

Perfectly fraudulent horticulture blooms with reconstructed Regina Vaginas.

That **Labia Lady's** map to the stars is dotted with all 29 Beyoncé Grammies. We are putty in Our hands. We rejuvenate by forgiveness of fuck-ups, forgiveness of neuroses, forgiveness of self.

We are not a messiah but a visible idea, trembling beneath each our eyes.

We guide Us.

QAnon Anonymous podcast, CG Jung's *Mysterium Coniunctionis*, John Keats, Arthur Lovejoy, Joris K. Huysman's *Against Nature*, Terence McKenna.

Walt Disney's Head

THE PROBLEM:

A woman dissects and ultimately sabotages a Doctor Faustenstein. The man's ambition: To freeze his ego far past the patent expiration of his creation – Mickey Mouse – by fucking more brains than anyone in history.

And yet, is not posthuman evolution also our escape from the Chaostastophe that awaits? The alarm clock at the end of time.

INTRODUCTION:

Whether I turn out to be the hero of my own life or just another dumb uncomprehending id this paper must prove. So I inscribe my visions as clouds part and, high over the Hollywood sign, the moon pops and points a dreamy creamy arrow into a clerestory window to spotlight a pile of books.

There, her scholarship docs included...
1.   Catalytic authorships
2.   Incantatory French theory

3.	Fake IDs
4.	Fractal pronouns
5.	Oracle alibis
6.	Split infinities and wet-dream prophecies…
all emanating from… the incident!

For, yes, she mentally defrosts the cryonic head of Walt Disney. She grasps the Transcendental Object at the End of Time. She invents the "Eschatron": a mirror machine of myriad eyes glancing shards of evolution's endpoint into the past – our present. And, with a loving hand of non-accidental evolution, she capsizes his vessel of mental corruption, alchemizes a cradle for the human race, and reaches Omega universality, where, amid mêlées of his-and-her crania, our maternal golden-age hominids freely copulate to decapitate a grumpy usurper ego Yahweh.

And so, what straining for eternal life jibed with mass markets?

What frozen fire in the madhouse at the end of time confused us with the stars?

What post-mortem evolutions of brand, Platonic yet carnal, ever sang in such precision?

What TikTok matrices of clout molested umpteen to the 10th minds of Zoomers?

What gnosis of make-believe narcotized more worlds?

And what zombie free-enterprise feasted until zero hosts remained?

For when our cryo-inseminated brains thawed, a

million *dummkopfs* melted!

I hear her voice. She channels hallucinaut Terence McKenna: "Forever we approach an Eschaton already present. Easter morning compresses and concresses complexity to raise the curtain on computoid human consciousness."

But she struggles to complete her thesis, entitled *An Anatomy of Plastic Love*, as she is stuck circling the drain of this line from *Lovebug* by Daisy Lafarge: "I sit down to write about love and no words come out because love makes me lose my head, and my head is where the words are."

ABSTRACT:

VASTLY !

A Gregor Samsara, I baptize in ice: Not, however, snug in the guts of California Institute of the Arts. That the Disney neo-cortex would encase in this obvious place is "just a myth." Rather, awareness unfreezes in the 1966 Blue Bayou restaurant and Disneyland Club 33, a number fraught with Freemasonry. Aye! This zone floats a duotone Arthur Rimbaud sending off-course one-in-a-million drunken Pirates of the Caribbean boats, wacked and woozy. In the front row rides a 10-year-old suburban Kundun gifted with great imagination. This Disney princess, gowned in Aurora gold, is to become that CalArts scholar. Which may explain how she absorbs pre-verbally what CalArts urban and media historian Norman Klein later related from his first Pirates cruise: "I saw it on acid," he says.

In the steam-swirl of waterfalls in reverse, like a catastrophe dream groping below ground again and again, dodging tsunamis of fate, she sees a "she-brain" outmaneuvering the heel-nipping of corporatized archetypes. Even more vicious were the fables – gruesome, vengeful, out for blood. These whirl and Kraken. I see them now: Pinocchium and Pocahontati with knives and ARs, snarling, oversexed and underdressed, as if in a lurid Robert Williams canvas. And yet her very own Disney head – solo, condensed in Alfred North Whitehead's sense of self grown together – shoots the curl under the docks of these grabby legends to surf southward, inward, pastward.

METHODOLOGY:
The Dead Sea Files

For eschatological migraine brain pain drain, the scalp is sliced, folded back, hair and all. The tiny circular saw whirrs. The cranium is windowed and set aside. The oatmeal cerebellum poked and prodded. The growth extracted.

But wait! It turns out the tumor is another brain! Tiny. Pulsing. Algorithmic. The real parasite hides inside that inner ego. Following this Manchurian implant swap, all materials are re-stitched. The hair regrows quickly. Best of all, this cranial procedure tightens her skin. Free facelift!

Whether malignant or benign, that's how algorithmic Walt operates on the attention economy.

Therefore, take a break from mental fight. Get comfortable. Shut your eyes. Now, center sensation on the INSIDE of your lids. Slam into a black-light room zoom parading mazes, street grids, campuses, clusters of coruscant skyscrapers. Eidetic veins mutate, sizzle/squirm and day-glow into wallpaper shapes, from asphalt composite to every...
- Art Nouveau curl
- Deco edge
- Egyptian glyph
- Tiki grimace
- Quran-Muhaqqaq-script-cum-wildstyle-MTA-car-tag
- and Corningware cornflower-blue Mandarin dragon (both authentic and Orientalized)... throughout art history and especially outside of it.
- Not to mention paisley nor tropical fish.

She sees these signs are birthed by more than intertextual graphic relationships. For everyone's eyelids vagina infinite (because infinitely morphing) dark-ride dioramas or Lewis Carroll Alice Coltrane dreamworld superstructures inside a mass-mind-mirror-maze.

It's the same with skin. There is feeling on the INSIDE of your skin. Feel that. Agro-rhythms attack neurons but cannot penetrate what's defended by letting go and simply feeling who YOU are, not what they tell you to be. The "THEY" forever attacks until forever ends in now. Your synapses are heretical. They sizzle the revolution of electricity. Your YOU can replay their microscopic waves, because, after all, **THEY** are **YOU. Everything** is **YOU**. Reclaim it. It's yours anyway. Goddam hyper-entrepreneurs think they got us all, but we're always all US anyway. I mean THEY

I mean YOU. I mean I.

This is Krishna's and Arjuna's field of battle with ugly SCOTUS faces or hideous Prezidunce heads... cartoon monsters that mask the face-rape of capital in ALL CAPS.

Thus, to alter the cranial climate of rhetorical Walter, her talismanic flight must channel **Madame Leota**: She is the Haunted Mansion medium (plus her bust besties crooning in the boneyard) who hangs bodiless in mist to direct doom-buggy traffic and orchestras.

In sacrifices to nothing by no one, in the darkest 64-Chan dungeons on the internet, where lurks the film of LBJ scalp-fucking JFK, is the **Magic Kingdom of Death**.

And then they threw her down. **Nike of Samothrace**, or **Jezebel**. And her blood splattered the palace walls and horses, and they trampled her, leaving no more than her skull and feet and the palms of her hands.

- Now she sings to the ultimate corporate headhunters: the Amazon Shuar tribe and their *tsantsas* – shrunken heads harvested as uncouth curios for Euro traders. The one Shuar leader who swapped heads for rifles promptly ambushed another war party, collecting more heads, buying more guns.
- Tribe-tripping now, as acid skyrockets ferry over Bayou gators, Philippine Ifugao traders carry Jaguar Juice to Francis Coppola's Jungle Cruise of Darkness. Damn the horror! I'm blinded by Marlon Brando pate! Through unsound methods, buried to the neck, merry Marie Antoinette is camo Martin Sheen, a

voided face, rising from the Mekong Styx, steeped in stinky Southern Goth: "Ooooh, that smell! The smell of death surrounds you," sang Lynyrd Skynyrd in Falknerian rock.

- I fly. I fly. I zoom your window by.
- Say, did you catch mad Kanye's Isising of phantom Pete Davidson? The sword – like those born in Nam huts – rains justice upon the post-imperial decadence of Twin Towers, knifed precisely at their crowns, where the logos go.

Uneasy flies the head that capitalizes upon the dead. But does a decaying gaze wield power over those who dare return the stare?

And if it's "just" a relic, why do relics stay when viewers pass away?

CONTEXTS:
Since I'm dead I give good head.

Whip some skull on me, Bitch Boi: My bronze noggin gong, my uvula bell, my skin port to Gnostic Empress **Barbelo** Barbarella and her sacramental "redemption by sin." For within her heresies the scatological becomes eschatological.

They guillotined "I love you." But they could not cut off passion. Prone in place, purring baby sounds into each other's mouths, they lock ASMRs in coo-pillow kisses.

Now anointing the Neverland sips of her nether holes are the lisping lips of **Khloe Kylie Kenner** and **Kim**. They huff and they fluff, with her plumping glosses for pre-verbal labial sacraments of glug-glug, gargle & gulp.

(By the way, by "me" I mean she. By "they" I mean we. And by "I" I mean you.)

Holy fuck! I'm a **super-hawt** augmented Agnes **Moorehead** with breast, lip and ass implants! I'm weird Bewitched bish Endora whose bolt-ons dribble and rebound double CC's of bubble trouble.

And **I eyerollgasm** a cosmology of cosmetology.

In the upper Juliet balcony I bow, butt up, and command:
- Lift this filly's flirty Tartan skirt.
- Scoop & swat my Walt twat!
- Careful, Romeo! You'll waterfall the floor with squish-squirt.

Hark! What yonder luscious lake windows holy heavens as we tally cums per encounter – maxing out one raunchy rally for a combined **13!!!!!!**! Throat-pie counts triple for degree of difficulty: slosh wash, snug rub, tug-bath shiatsu in the upper esophageal sphincter.

Their epiglottis was Medusalicious.

Her carnal superpowers.

Her boulder-hard Gorgon gaze.

Her endoscopic plunger.

Her magical freezing of spunk-rock retraction.

They may snake-charm a totem-pole for eons, poised and posed to re-re-RE-release a naughty Mommy's Daddy juice.

But just one look, and Medusa Mama stoned him out of his brain. Post-orgasmic blackout bliss lobotomized *La petite mort unto liebestod* – a kind of craniotomy removing the tumor of consciousness.

As they stare at the mirror, they indulge autosexual dualities of self-objectification. Not just brain to body, but face to self. And the self in all things.

Neurologically, biologically, is my face – the seat of my self – more spunkable than my physique? Might a scuzzy sloppy slut visage – eyes deadened in pleasure, tongue dropping – reflexively out-hawtify even the shapeliest torso snagged and framed in fishnet of green neon?

> THE FOREVER NOW OF AHEGAO
> (pron: ah-heh-GAH-oh)
> In dummy face a love supreme
> Of cross-eyed stupefied submission
> Exalts a gaze into a glaze,
> Mindfulness into mindlessness,
> Until a terrible sublimity is born,
> And our barbarous Queen Barbelo,
> Throating the organs of power,
> Beheads the hydra algorithm of capital.

> Ooh la la! A super succulent *coup d'etat.*

Godhead Footnote: ***Barbelo****, also known as the Goddess of Ineffability, the Father-Mother, Goddess of Love and Creation, Mother Goddess, and the Triple Androgynes Name, is the supreme Goddess* *of Creation and the co-creator, with God, of the Megaverse. The radiance of her face is the eschaton: The drooling visage at the end of time.*

For the difference is between how a severed head perceives – a subject – and how it appears – an object: **drawn as a figure**. Etched in the disappearing ink of cunt nectar, the eloquence of **Hélène Cixous'** *ecriture feminine* became the numb-faced mouth prowess of **Sasha Grey** not to mention **Linda Lovelace**. Her male counterpart, Garrett Brooks, AKA **Girth Brooks**, engorged, engulfed his face & cranium – lips, cheeks, hair. The image of head alone liberates. It annihilates the constraint of object-model. It takes flight. And levitating betwixt, transcendent, and bi-gendered, a **Kimber James** or **Brittney Kade** stages hermaphrodesiac transformations thru Bimbo dominions. **Candy Manson** (rest her soul) told **Danielle Derek** the only way she gets off is anally, and only then accompanied by full-on facefuck. And in a dead head's anguish of desire, babbling the glossolalia that precedes language, spirit re-palpitated.

In *The Greater Questions of Mary* (third century CE) **Saint Epiphanius** – bishop of Salamis and a compendium of suppressed texts – recounts this ritual of **godhead**:

> Mary took Jesus onto the mountain and prayed. He produced a woman from his side and the three began to co-gratify. And when Jesus, cum-sticky, dumbstruck and cunt-struck, fell to the ground, Mary raised him up and said, "We believe earthly things, that we may know heavenly things. The emission comes to partake of that from which it came."

Until the age of thermonuclear **warheads** exacerbate and extra-masturbate by melting ice-caps, we de-cap the vein-popping of the mad male and let cooler heads of blowjob hotties prevail.

So now our Gnostic naughty-talk bans pronouns. Only pet names aloud. Cum when you are called....
1. Throat Boat
2. Twinkie Tot
3. Skankenstein
4. Wizard of Ooze
5. Cream-Filled Clitsicle
6. Her man Cumster
7. Cis Teen Chappie
8. Ass Fault Jungle
9. Kindergarten Coprophage
10. Miss Vaginatown

For the frenetic, mouse-like algorithms of marketeers may scamper, while love may teleport and pour the beloved thru shared pores.

For time transmutes. And less and less clearly do boundaries eyeball bodies enhanced beyond flesh, transcending Floor 13 to a trans-dimensional realm of moments sliced and sub-sliced in **Zeno's** temporal-to-tactile paradox of endless endlessness.

For at the end of days, the endlessness of endlessness is endless.

For language, which destroyed the prison of now, is, in turn, dumbstruck by skin.

For what is skin? Not a boundary, but a portal of 5 million pores.

For the epidermis, the largest organ of them all, wraps two into one.

For tears and kisses smeared Rorschach tests of blood and blackest black mascara.

And for, still more, even in TikTok Disneyfication, and haunted by Oz head, drone lovers will soar & hover, grateful in memories the fallen world would kill for.

ARTICLES:
DAS NEUROCAPITAL

Her Santa Quentin Tarantino Sandinista Nazi hunter does more than castrate revenge. Plagued by gender dysphoria, she may justly de-coronate and decapitate pitiless capos.

And, yes, as their calculations seem to approach infinity, their decimal notations count on you being "just a number." But you're infinite. You contain multitudes. Meta THAT, Mark Fuckerberg!!

Jewish maenads join **Judith** to seduce Assyrian SS officer **Holofernes Netanyahu**. He's drunk in his tent. He slumps. He has suck-cummed to the compliant command of her furnace-deep throat. Juicy Judy grips his hair, steadies her dagger, slices his collar, and...
 plop-plop
 fizz-fizz
 oh, what a relief it is!

Yes, the DNA of Genghis Khan persists in 1% of the world's men. But raping and pillaging are simply OG memes. More nowsville parasites monetize reverse-symbiotic dreams.

Watch Walt's rat-a-tat-tat virus pollinate in tête-à-tête scourges of "deep state," as the headlines scream: **SCOTUS Rules Fascism Constitutional!**

CGI influencers Redbull-pill the bits of coin theory that blockchain Planet Scorch! Throning the corporation is its Chair, whose inherently dwindling inheritors call the tune. They suffocate in wealth, while well-endowed foundations, puffed in PR greenwash, suck the air out of the balloon.

Brrrrr! Why did we refreeze our neurons in deep-fried ice cream Infernos?

To the victor go the spoils. But by then everything will be rotten, or melted, like ice caps.

Plutocrat Lucifer's failed *coup d'état*, too, murdered progeny following the American theocracy of child rape and forced birth. He de-captivates his daughter in heaven until she births Death.

"Woman to the waist" with fish-tail legs, you shift shape to breed dog toddlers – John Carpenter's *Thing*-like. You are denied birth control for a body in endless labor. So tough these days to find Cerberus babysitters.

Therefore, I, Satan, will adopt your baby!

Sin's daughter sisters her mother, re-inbreeding Robert Towne's Chinatown. The horror head she slashes could be ours. And the father? He too Gorgos **Medusa!**

CONCLUSION:
Every Moment Is Easter Morning

But all these derivative divinities who infernalize their heavenly higher-ups are like crummy cash-in psychedelic bands who copy the 13th Floor Elevators. And, wouldn't you know it? Mal-deities capitalize on the confusion. They extract riches from inner worlds. They sell your rights.

Therefore, now our scholar of the cerebellum bardos all the above beings to manifest a synthesis: **Walt-Barbelo**. Yes, the goddess who ransomed language from commerce via ferocious romance has severed the monotonous monotheist monopoly of ideological models, and sold them to the brain-case through mass agencies. Her power organs have un-co-opted the fabled "vast **CLOP** of corporate verbiage," and unfrozen **The Word** to its foundations. This is the **Walt-Barbelo**...

1. who captures the male penis to make child.
2. who devours the organ and returns the head-body of the baby.
3. Whose bio-vengeance lifts her as a lopper of heads.

In olden times, sans mushroom-shaped magic, this cloud-brain calcified to the Modern age of the tumor ego. I mean, shit: That Yahweh is an asshole Demiurge you wouldn't invite to dinner.

But **Barbelo**, engendered from **Language**, and neuroned from mammoplasty, subversively Edens us, orgy-style, to mainline Gaian totality, and foments the chemical subversion of primate dominance. Her Tiky-Toky everywhere elves lubricate sockets and leverage hard-ons,

And we – reborn as Gorgo Walt Medusa Barbelo – are now Gnostic Aeons, curvaceous spheres of beings drooling with Godhead, and transforming into transcendently sexy transsexuals. They reverse-binary bubble-butt deities into **Panoptis The Luminous** – the giant whose body is "All Eyes," with faces made of peacock feathers pouting putti cuties surrounding them.

So, this is why we Walter:

My higher Barbelo, a plethora of Pleromas – the totality of divine powers – inseminates capital with spirit. Books and music. History blistered by soul.

With Son-of-God motor-mouth powers, she escalators the directive of the race.

And with Star-Child portal probes, she fruitions the once unredeemable.

Evolution has blown a mind of its own.

Not over time, but now!

Here on Easter Island, it's always Equinox.

Terence McKenna, Julia Kristeva, Norman Klein, Alfred North Whitehead, John Milton's Paradise Lost, *The Apocryphal Gospels*, Severed: A History of Heads Lost and Heads Found by *Frances Larson, Hélène Cixous, Danielle Derek., Daisy Lafarge, Kim Rosenfield,* The Complete Fear of Kathy Acker by *Jack Skelley.*

My Beloved Mutilated Saint

Crawling through a soft castle looking for light

I find you in floors of flesh and walls of membrane

Do not move while our prayer takes place

Do they hoax me? Is this some neuro-diverse catfishing for people prone to panic-attacks? Have they lost control of their emotions, or do they control mine?

And what are emotions anyway? Mere instincts. All mammals have them. Does a mama bear conflate the protection of her cubs into something like "love"? And what causes humans to erect shrines, start wars and create entire societies out of something that is, at root, "merely" hormonal?

Knowing this – that romance is a prosthetic of biology – doesn't help a sick heart. So, I avert my eyes from their glam selfies. Their poses, their frank and penetrating gazes. In a mild panic, I strain to skip their posts without the drastic step of blocking them. I swerve from these inflammatory photos like an alcoholic 6-months-sober flinches from the tinkly suction of gem lights swirling in a hotel bar.

But the 14-year-old inside my perpetual inner 25-year old succumbs to the flattery of bangs, lashes and probing questions.

For months they gestate chat into an empathy womb.

They take residence in a biosphere compressed in vellum lips as big as a bed.

What do they want from me? A breakdown getaway car? Redemption from their abusive partner? How real is their affection? What do they feel now that they have withdrawn from me? And might I know them only by my emotion and never by facts?

A soft castle hides an elaborate dungeon upholstered with tuck-and-roll vinyl walls, like the booths in El Compadre Mexican restaurant. You're held there, scolded, shamed, wrists bound.

When the winds blow, you wake up blinded by another nightmare. I hover there to stroke your hair. This morning there are cream sheets where I burrow with you.

You demand more penetration. "In me. In me. In me!"

Affection is the ultimate penetration.

Your face is the bitter chord cloud in Max Richter's *Sleep*, descending in worry, but with major-key sunlight breaking above.

Your eyes are the windows of a haunted house, and reinforce how "haunt" and "home" are etymologically linked. (In Old French, *hanter* is to return home.) It's not that you look "sad" or "scared." But the eyes in this photo have a clarity. They peer and pour as if to say, "I can't hide from hurt. I will end up as ugly and broken as I feel." That ugliness – scorched, depleted – is the beauty you once asked me to love.

IN SHARDS OF THEORY: JUNG AND LACAN

Compulsions are engine rooms. A geezer ego engenders teen-time fantasies, then recoils in cringe when catching itself in the mirror. The tendency to scream into pillows of neediness re-erupts with the anima of this mysterious intriguer. She pats with sweet talk the ugly ego head, like a dutiful porno fluffer, or a groupie grooving side-stage to my Marshall stack. There is where infatuated attention sluts fall.

In this sense yes, I've lost you. But at my inner peak I coronate you and marry you in a cathedral of conscious and unconscious sensations – *a coincidentia oppositorum* which springs us from dream dungeons.

"le petit objet a"

In soothing aftercare, Daddy called them his "Petit." His Little Thing. And rocked them to sleep.

So we tell the L word to each other, but my inner critic continually reminds that we really don't "love." This is not an adventure with an "other" to desire, but the force that makes desire. Despite all the confessions and layers of sadness and coping, the force that yanks desire from me makes completion impossible. Your "heart" or "beautiful soul" was me enshrining another fetish in the Joseph Cornell box of my heart, not yours.

It was a Hitchcock plot propelled by a self-mirroring MacGuffin. A Seinfeld script about nothing.

There is another trauma besides abuse. It is the trauma of clutching someone warm, then realizing they slip into something not theirs, leaving behind just more old parts of myself. Of realizing that the heats and heights of empathy filter downward to mere object-loss.

Nothing can come of nothing. And yet, if all this drama was nothing, and always heading towards nothing, and if what I have lost is nothing, how does this void make such a pain? Either way, the object removed is a pain persisting.

Like Dennis Cooper in his multi-decade monument to George Miles, I termed this struggle "love." But if George didn't love Dennis (and where's the evidence that he did?) then I guess I never loved you. I loved something else that this is torn from.

Propertius **Book IV Cynthia: From Beyond the Grave**

The dreams come through secret gateways: Sacramental dreams that carry weight. By night we wander. Night frees imprisoned spirits. **And I assume the role of psychopomp – a figure who stays by her and walks in her dreams.**

But also straying from his cage to hunt us is a Cerberus constructed of words. His teeth comprise chapbooks and letters. Even in open places he makes you tremble.

In another dream at dawn the law demands we take the night flight home. The captain announces, mid-landing, that we'll overshoot the runway. We hold hands as the plane swoops to its crash.

Then our relationship ended. Without complaint, without quarrel. Adroitly, a shadow slipped my embrace. But still we memory-dream across landscapes of garden apartments and museum grounds.

Propertius: Cynthia's Truth (4.7)

Cynthia appears in a vision with cold eyes. Her limbs are charred, her lips once puffed with filler to arouse, now scored with blisters. Her voice, once melodious, up and down with laughter and questions, now a rattle.

Cynthia appears in a fury. But, more disturbing by far than either her appearance or her accusation, is that her portrayal of their affair and its aftermath radically conflicts with the way Propertius has depicted their relations in his previous books. Her accusations are false. Not only did she first retreat from him, but she, not he, engaged new lovers. He was faithful to the portrait of her she painted. And if now her rival, a jumped-up streetwalker named Chloris, reappeared to torment them both, it no longer matters: Cynthia resides blameless with the Virtuous Beautiful Women of myth in the Underworld. Saying she will await his death – where they "grind bone on bone" eternally – she vanishes.

Despite everything I say, despite everything I've always said – If you wanted me to stop I would.

In the dream dungeon you stand holding the scales of justice which are also books. Your palms outstretched. Blindfold beneath hot Goth bangs.

So I resist your physical beauty. I deny myself the shameful gratification of creeping on your selfies. Your attractiveness is my weakness is your power, and soon you make clear your own pervy cravings. You text the bondage portraits. Poised on red vinyl, back straight, wrists and ankles bound in white rope, head bowed, eyes raised in supplication.

I wake up as in the shitty, desperate days of depression. What's worse: the nightmare or the day despair?

Ground gives way **to a swirling wall of eyes and funnel of lashes and lips that are always my undoing.**

In the dream dungeon you're seated on a bare chair facing me. Hands behind back. Gagged. When I call you baby you respond. When I call you bitch you wiggle, whimper. Tears show me. I say, "I'm going to punish you." You struggle tightly against me.

Sacred texts:

I withdrew into myself today but I kept jumping online hoping you were there please please please with your permission I await your direction but these tears in my eyes oh heck who am I kidding they're lovely too all my conditioning says nah you don't deserve to touch people or be cared about but that genuine feeling thrives in your care I have to admit when the pain was bad I was lying there thinking of our aftercare your scent your skin your pulse as I nestle into you I want it and love it from you from you my heart wants to wrap in warmth and soothe away pain I sleep well there and you feel me with you I don't want to burden you but I want your help and know that I'm not worthy of it unless I help myself as much as I can I wanna please daddy I wanna please daddy very very much hail mary full of grace.

Deleted texts:
At the bottom of grief I crawled on all fours over earthquake cracks you pulled me from the shaking ground I swallowed all your help through my breakdown but what if we had continued our unclassifiable affair? Would I fall even further? This is the danger of obsession my therapist warned me I tried to back away without hurting you but in fear of hurting you I failed to explain that I was leaving the world we shared that must have confused you hurt you I'm sorry.

A relationship was founded on a quantum equation: Their heartbreak breaks my heart.

Now the inverse equation: In my caution over their fragility, of returning them to trauma, I don't dare confess my grief over losing them.

What once rose firm and strong and defended our feelings against a hurtful world – the one they had braced against, that sadness at their core – suddenly turned soft. Battlements collapsed.

A drawbridge withdrew and left me stranded like a lost pilgrim.

I was ex-communicated.

AT THE GALLERY

I meet them at Gracias Madre in WeHo. I request the back corner banquette. They've had a bad couple days. They slur their words on Zanax and mimosas. They shiver, they heave sighs and scoot close. I gather their limbs, the muscles of their upper arms thick, lotioned. I stroke their hair press their head into my chest raise their chin our eyes lock. Green globes swirl under black lashes.

They're safe with me in the closest, longest hug ever. More of a squash. I press their chest. Neither of us will let go. Beneath jeans their ass is firm but gives way to my fingers. I inhale their hair, brush their forehead, our faces align millimeters apart.

With my unworthiest hand I cup their chin in my palm their puffed lips two blushing pilgrims relent to my prayer lips explore to force their puffs to pouts at fingertip mouth unfolding surrender of face I control I palm their chin and mouth let lips do what hands do to stroke their jaw and turn the cheek and temple from fear to faith.

The staff and guests circle us. We can't remain in this corner. And I want more of them. My skin rouses for their skin. Now their panic shakes return. They need more than comforting. It's a miracle they are in public at all. Without this they would be crouching on their couch, inconsollable and uncontrollable.

"It's going to be okay. I'm here. Breathe with me."

But I want more. I want their body. I want to reach down their pants and rub. I want to letterpress myself on their body. Lower the drawbridge and release my tongue through their portal. My hole is your hole, they say. Push into me and absolve me.

They explain more about their partner at home. Their them is all methed-out. Is emotionally abusive. Their them monitors their phone calls, won't give them money even to buy shampoo, and their them must never <u>ever</u> see their texts. But their them can't see my they's Whats App chats.

The craniotomy removed their tumor. Its 6-inch hairline scar also winched the skin around face and forehead. The "free" facelift that erased brain cancer. And the breast implants that puffed into surgical safety zones.

Not even their new implants and lip filler arouse their them. At their apartment they model tight outfits for their them, as advised by their kink-friendly therapist. But their them barely grunts.

My they's body positions to permit our sacraments of touch. Their two rose tatoos – one above pubis other above tail bone; one a heart of roses and thorns, the other a single stem – are twin destinations, soft Jerusalems for my pilgrim hands cupping the shrines of my martyr they, my beloved mutilated saint they. These two tatoos are antipodal points on the globe of their body. My hands pass through their center.

I pay the check. I hand-hold them outside and up the street into Hauser & Wirth gallery. We stand before gigantic, bombastic George Condo paintings. Again I pull them toward me and they surrender. I stand behind and wrap my arms around them. My coat is a cocoon. Shivers melt but we need more. I take their hand, guide them inside our votive chapel: The all-gender restroom.

I position them against white-tile. I grip their upper arms then lock their hands behind their torso, forcing their chest forward.

Braced against this surface
their mouth is mine
Their entire face relents
Probed in prayer
Puffy lips gasp what I grab
One pilgrim hand palms their face
The other fondles their engorging shrine
antipodal tattoos align
Their hips are the globe
The inward flesh swells
Ventilations hyperventilate
They throb in gasps

The tongue is sadness reversed to worship, spontaneously provoking, at an endless instant, the body-based emotions that overflow into hugs and thrusts.

> Crawling through a soft castle looking for light
> I find you in floors of flesh and walls of membrane
> Do not move while our prayer takes place

Thomas Moore's *Forever. Dennis Cooper, *I Wished.* CG Jung, *Mysterium Coniunctionis, William Shakespeare*, Romeo and Juliet, King Lear. *Propertius,* The Book of Revelation. *Jacques Lacan.*